A Cluster of Petals

(A Collection of short stories)

BY
Oluwaseyi Adebola

First published 2019 by SO4L Educational consultancy Nigeria limited.

Edited by Oluwayomi S. Oladunjoye, associate professor of English as a second language and Dean of student affairs, OOU Ago-Iwoye, Nigeria.

The bonus story *'How to be a Maga'* is based on a true-life experience. Some names and identifying details have been changed to protect the privacy of individuals.

DEDICATION

For Funmilola

For Family

For Friends

Finally, you have an inkling of what was probably going on in my head all those days I stared at the ceiling with glazed eyes: talking hands, poetic shoes and monsters, all dancing around in mirth, enveloped by a mist of satire.

This work is for you and others like me, around the world, who build worlds and worlds in their heads of things, not as they are, but all the infinite ways they can be.

I dedicate this enigmatic cluster of wild and varied petals to you...

A Cluster of Petals

Grandpa once told me a magical story
About an old vase he used to have
It contained a cluster of petals, he said
With a silvery tear at the corner of his eye,
And wisps of thinning, greyish hair on his head.

Grandpa told me the petals were beautiful
Covered in a swathe of dazzling colours
That bounced off the sunlight into his humdrum room.
They were the different spectra of the rainbow
They were the warm feeling of summer.

Grandpa said life was like that vase
Different flowers, different shades; different colours, different days
Intricately linked together like web
And if you viewed the vase with the eyes of a bee
Then the petals are like a song of honey - or a portrait of grace.

CONTENTS

2 RIGHT HANDS

A

Two little raps delivered in quick succession sounded at the door. Two long legs clad in blue denim lazily dragged themselves from their comfort zone atop a little wooden stool because their owners needed them to get to the door. Thousands of miles from home and on the thirteenth floor in an impressively looking tower in Barbican centre, London, Tokunbo knew just who to expect at the door. He also knew what clothes the person would be wearing.

A smirk registered on his lips. He opened the door gingerly, his left hand adjusting the volume of his television set.

Waheed Sadiku, mobile handset in hand, and smiling like he controlled half of the World Bank walked in calculated steps into the dimly lit apartment.

"The only dog…" He waited for Tokunbo to complete the statement for the umpteenth time. In a majestic tone, Tokunbo added, "That even the wolves see and tremble"

They shook themselves hard and warmly ending with the usual customary pat on the back.

Tokunbo directed Waheed with a motion of his left hand to a leather sofa directly facing the T.V.

"Anything...?" Tokunbo asked half expecting the already familiar answer. Waheed waved it off with a wave of his hand.

"Thanks though" He added courteously. "So, what's up?" Waheed asked, ready for what he knew would be a long chit-chat. You could not expect anything short of extraordinary in that department when it came to Tokunbo. He could summon a lengthy discussion from a statement carelessly uttered.

"Oh, I've been watching TV all day, you know, just lazing around...you know, that sort of thing.

Waheed dwelled a bit what the television had to offer. Tokunbo was one of the few people who still insisted on satellite television despite the excellent job the local TV stations were doing. The television was tuned to BBC where an overly enthusiastic reporter was doing her best to impress her superiors...

*"The Jews often refer to the Holocaust as '**Shoah'**, gotten from the Hebrew word for "catastrophe" or "total destruction".* The young female reporter smoothened her hair as the wind seemed desperate to blow it off her head. She deepened her look into the cameras for maximum 'reporter effect'.

*"Holocaust itself was probably gotten from the Greek word **holo**, meaning whole and **caustos,** meaning burned, and I really cannot think of a more all-encompassing term, because an attempt was made to exterminate this wonderful people, their culture and their name. An attempt was literarily made to pluck out their very souls and burn it forever. And it was almost a success story. But why..."*

"So?" Waheed asked indifferently. Tokunbo however seemed to be absorbed in the reporter's use of words because he remained still for a few moments, a frown budding on his face.

"I learnt the Government of West Germany made a couple of compensatory efforts...It's simply a pity man has always been on a desperate mission to destroy the world around. And now that He is almost half done, he thinks, why not go for life itself?"

"...er...You're right...or...well, not really?" Tokunbo appeared not to have recovered from the reporter's spells. Waheed could not imagine the story been the real reason for his friend's captivation. After all, it had been around for decades and he knew Tokunbo was not really a Hi-story kind of person, especially when he had his own story to ruminate upon. He was thirty years old without as much as a fling or casual girlfriend. Or maybe it was not really as pathetic as it looked.

Tokunbo had sat down by his side and touched Waheed lightly to bring him back.

"Actually..." he started. Waheed braced himself up for a long speech. "It is hardly an issue of reparations or compensations. Screw that." He stuck up his middle finger for emphasis.

"How much does the warmth of a loved one cost? How much is life? I think it all boils down to this issue of competition...em...as postulated by...was it Darwin or Lerwin..." Tokunbo scratched his head in an attempt to dig into Biology lessons he had almost fifteen years ago.

"Competition?" Waheed had initially thought he would just go through the whole process and not have to add anything, but as usual, he was wrong. Tokunbo was second only to Sururat, his fiancée, in bringing him out of 'mute' mode. That was why he always turned up here at evenings when he was bored and tired of the European customary solitary lifestyle. He knew Tokunbo was up to the task of enchanting his day with distracting chatter.

The issue of competition just did not register. Tokunbo appeared to have read his thoughts.

"You don't get it, do you?" Tokunbo did not wait for an answer.

What the heck? It was hardly a question in the first place.

"The issue is this; everybody seems to have this crazy idea locked up in the recesses of their minds that they are better off than the next person, and that the world would be a much more comfortable place if it had more of them in it. We seem to think that we have

the solution to the world's problems at our finger tips and are ever so eager to impress these supposed solutions on the person next to us. Look at religion for instance..." Tokunbo however stopped suddenly when he saw Waheed's muscle tense. Religion was one thing that never got into their lengthy discussions, Waheed being a stout Muslim, and Tokunbo being a Christian, a passive one notwithstanding.

Not being one to end a debate without a sense of completion, Tokunbo fired on.

"I sincerely believe this same innate attribute we all have to constantly compete with one another is responsible for the wars, religious conflicts et cetera...at least to some extent"

Tokunbo folded his arms and rested his back, satisfied he had done justice to the topic. He likened his room to one of those ancient Greek courts where men were reputed to have simply sat down and discussed everything, from philosophy, to the reason why soil was on the ground and the sky in the air, and not the other way around. He waited patiently for Waheed's contribution. When it finally came, it was desperate to divert the discussion at a tangent.

"Anthony called you, right?"

Those words were like a blow carefully aimed and delivered and they hit a very soft spot on Tokunbo's emotions.

"This has nothing to do with Tony, and yes, he called...yesterday, in the morning" Tokunbo tried his best to maintain his breathing rate.

Anthony's square face resurfaced in his mind. As usual it was laden with that stupid look. What would he not do to remove *that look*? Anthony always wore a knowing look; like he knew the question you were about to ask even before it got formed in your mind. And maybe Tokunbo would not have cared much if not for the fact that Tony really did know the answers to the questions their teachers threw at them, and the questions kept on coming, and coming. The stream of answers did not run dry either. The story goes thus: A little over fourteen years ago, Tokunbo and Waheed were classmates in a Federal Government College back in Nigeria. Then along came Tony...Out of the blues, the boy appeared as a new student when they were in the first year of their senior secondary school and Tokunbo's academic life was never the same again. The 1st in his reports were gradually turning to 2nd, the same way Moses turned water red in the Bible. The 'Dear' that had almost taken over as his name on the lips of his teachers steadily got replaced by his full names, and Tony just stayed there on top of the class, not even going on a single break, taunting Tokunbo as often as he could with that his look...

"I imagine you will find it hard to believe, but really, this has nothing to do with Tony."

"Alright, I guess I believe you. And I must say, you made a lot of

sense. Provided of course that..."

Tokunbo's cold stare stopped him in his tracks. Waheed laughed heartily, Tokunbo joining him in no time at all. They talked late into the night, discussing everything from politics in Nigeria to Tokunbo's pathetic romantic life like that was all they were born to do. They tried to imagine that somewhere else on the Earth, these issues were playing out in the lives of other people. Maybe even children. They considered themselves philosophers dissecting the microcosms of life and living.

Just like the famous Greek courts...

****

B

Pathfinders' nursery and primary school was the only school at Barbara estate. It consisted of a pair of five storey buildings.

Each one painted with the theme colours of the school; creamy white and a clear navy blue. The school had a playgroup class all the way to the last class in the 6-3-3-4 system of the country for the primary level, primary six. The primary three class had the greatest number of pupils and hence generated the most attention. This was the reason why the class was divided into two different arms, the lil' robins and the lilies. Roy Jaiyeola was a prominent member of the lil' robins.

Roy was a boy of 8 years, shy looking with pronounced ears and a little too big for his age. He was the last child of his parents, and hence, over pampered. Like many other families in his classy estate, his consisted of his dad, mum, and just three kids. He had two elder brothers, both of whom were well ahead of him in years.

Philip, his eldest brother was twenty-two years of age and in his final year at the university. Samson on the other hand was 17 years old and had just graduated from secondary school.

"Roy" miss Mary, standing in front of the classroom, called gently.

"Yes, auntie"

"Hope you have distributed the excursion letter to every single person in the class. I do not want anyone complaining that he wasn't given the letter and hence couldn't pay for the excursion on that day. I hear the zoo is a very beautiful place and one I'm sure you all will like to visit. Remember, we will be leaving next week Friday. Do not forget to ask your parents for some warm clothing and a couple of bananas to give the monkeys. See you all tomorrow. Bye." A boy gingerly raised his hands to call the attention of the teacher, but she briskly walked out of the class in a rush completely oblivious of him.

This boy was Richard.

Richard sat two seats away from Roy. His father was a driver at one of the big banks in the state. He walked smartly to Roy's seat just before Roy stood up, about to leave.

"Roy"

Roy looked up to see who was calling. When he saw Richard's innocent looking face, he shifted his focus back to packing his books.

"Roy" Richard called again a little bit louder. When Roy still did not answer, he tapped him lightly on his shoulder.

"Will you not hear me out?"

Roy pushed Richard's hand away from his shoulder before he responded.

"And when did I tell you I had gone deaf? Or must I look at you before I hear what you are saying?"

"Oh sorry" Richard quickly apologized.

"I thought you did not hear me. I just wanted to ask you for the excursion letter. It's like you forgot to give me my own copy."

"Sorry, there's none for you" Roy said grudgingly to Richard's amazement.

"What do you mean by none for me? I thought Auntie Mary said something about you giving everybody the letter" Richard enquired further, still not losing his temper.

"Well, that's what she said, not what I did. In any case, I do not think you will be able to afford it. I hear the gate fee is very high, and not just for anybody." Roy said this waving his fingers at Richard's tattered school uniform.

"How could you say such a mean thing?" Jane asked irritably. She had been carefully observing the scenario from behind. Jane was one of the few girls in the class who never seemed to mind been associated with Richard.

"Is it because He did better than you in the mathematics test?

In any case, it isn't like you failed. After all, you certainly can't be the best all the time."

"Shut your traps!" Roy snapped back at the girl. He opened his mouth to say something else when Richard suddenly spoke with tears in his eyes, "I pray this class captain position is taken from you and given to someone else who will be humbler and less discriminatory." He turned his back to Roy and went to his seat to continue crying. Jane ran to comfort him, shoving Roy out of the way. Roy was not fazed. He hissed and continued his journey out of the classroom.

"Both of you are simply jealous." He hissed again, more vehemently.

"After all, if you wanted the position, then you might as well have asked for it. Right now, it is all mine, and none of you barking wolves can snatch it from me." He banged the door behind him.

The school usually closed at about 2.20 pm. The driver then waited for about 25 minutes for all the students to be seated before he drove off. Roy's home was the last on the street, so he always got home by 3pm, every day.

"Good afternoon sir." Roy said to his dad, who had come to open the door for him. Roy's father was a chief executive of an insurance company; hence he chose to come home whenever he liked.

"How was school today, lil' soldier?" Mr. Jaiyeola asked, trying to lift Roy up. Roy declined and shrugged his shoulders.

"I am no longer a small boy dad, remember? Please don't do this in front of my friends."

"Whatever" His dad replied. "Even after you are married, you'll still be my baby"

Roy was about to protest but stopped when Samson walked in.

"Gooday Pops" He greeted. He walked up to Roy and ruffled his hair before heading for his room.

"Samson" Mr. Jaiyeola quickly called out.

"Sir"

"I just remembered. When you finish eating, I want you to take the car and deliver the package in your room to Mr. Emmanuel."

"Alright" Samson said.

"Daddy" Roy tugged his dad's sleeves. "Sir?" His dad replied jokingly.

"Why don't you send me on errands with the car?" Roy asked.

"That's because you can't drive" His dad answered softly.

"But you can teach me, just like you taught Samson, right?"

"No, you are too young." This time, it was Samson who answered.

He had heard Roy's question while he was going to his room, and being a familiar one, he came to give a familiar answer. One his dad has not been able to say till date.

"What makes you think I am too young? It's like you have forgotten that I am eight years old. Moreover, I'll be nine in four months' time."

"Well that's the way it is. Piece of advice from me, don't set your hopes high. I learnt how to drive when I was 16 years old. I don't see your case been any different"

"Stop it!" Roy screamed. He hated it when Samson treated him as an inferior person. As long as they were all boys, whatever was good for one of them was good for the other two.

"Dad, he's wrong, isn't he?" Roy wanted his dad to take his side.

"About?" Mr. Jaiyeola pretended not to know what Roy was talking about. "...Me not learning to drive till I am sixteen."

Mr. Jaiyeola simply nodded to satisfy Roy. He knew Roy would pester him for hours explaining why he was no longer a little boy if he did not tell him what he wanted to hear.

"Besides, I am the class captain of my class. My case **should** be different." Roy added as he dashed into his room.

Mr. Jaiyeola dared not mention to Roy that he was class captain because one Miss Mary did him a favour.

The telecom buzzed like a baby begging to be fed by its mother. Delicately painted fingers picked them up gingerly.

"Sir?"

The voice on the other end was tough, but the words adroitly delivered, the way CEO's learnt to sound "Please I would like to have the reports on my desk before the end of the day" Sarah Jaiyeola looked at the leather wristwatch on her hand. She had about two hours to this time Mr. Akpabio had in mind. Mr. Udoh Akpabio was the ultimate 'Grass to grace story' Born to poor parents whose farms had been destroyed by the very crude oil that fed the country where they lived pretty much lived from hands to mouth. Like Chief Edet Akpabio had taught Moses Akpabio who tried to teach Mr. Udoh Akpabio, children came from God, and where in their numbers a measure of the success of a proper Warri man. So, in the midst of fervent poverty, the children kept coming out, and numbered 21 the last time Udoh set his legs in that *cursed village* as he would normally call it. He however had one thing on his side- an almost obsessive determination to break from the stench of poverty that had come to be associated with his family name, and somehow through thick and thin, he was now the executive manager of a company whose drivers earned more than some doctors. It was only natural that Sarah came to respect this man. Her eyes travelled to the corner of her table where the kits for the report she was about to prepare lay. They however passed by a picture of family that seemed to vividly stand out on her polished desk, and that was because of her eyes. Her mind wandered again, carefully trailing behind her eyes. Her husband in his 5-foot 11 frame and infectious smile sat beside her on the sofa. If there were going to be a remake of that Indian film whose title was 'opposites attract', they would probably consider she and her husband for lead roles. He was laidback and histrionic; she was the ideal egghead who almost never talked. Their kids towered behind them like a mother hen over her chicks, Philip, Samson, and Roy whom her eyes settled on. His eyes were quizzing, and his mouth was upturned, ready to make the kind of sharp comments that threw defendants in a law court off their seats. If she was born a boy, he was an exact picture of what she would have looked like. Sharp, driven, and in control.

Where he was different was in his thirst to govern, and of course the Naira rain his roofs provided. Her eldest sons were even more different. Philip prayed all the time while Samson only had ears for rap music. Philip loved mathematics and was desperate to become the most successful banker that ever lived; Samson simply loved James Hardley Chase novels and was somewhat confident every good thing would come his way in good time; Philip was not dumb, it was just that he decided to almost never speak; Samson on the other hand was talkative and smooth at it. He was motivational speaker material...

Sarah always marvelled at how people so different could live together as a family, but somehow, they pulled it through successfully, and she guessed that was the way it was in many other homes. More importantly, like her husband would usually say, with a calm smile on his lips, that was what made the world go around. It was the reason the moon came out in the night, and left early enough to allow the sun its own grand entry; It was why the world turned out to be spherical and not some sharp-edged planet over which ships could fall; It was the reason the world was beautiful...

Somehow, her left wrist found a way to show her the time. Automatically, she logged out of the section of her mind that only wanted to daydream and entered the section that just loved to work. Her right hand grabbed a stack of files and instantaneously started shuffling through them.

Roy's most dreaded hour of the day was 10.00pm. That was when he had to go to bed. Incidentally, there were always a lot of interesting programs on DSTV at this time. Worse still, Samson always chuckled as their Mum ushered Roy to his bedroom. Roy's mum was an accountant in a major oil firm. She always left home at 5.30 in the morning, long before Roy opened his eyes and never returned till about 9 in the night. She therefore always treasured the little time she had to spend with her kids before they retired to bed.

Mrs. Jaiyeola ushered Roy into his bedroom then lovingly tucked him into bed. Like her mom and Grandma always did, he said a short prayer with him before leaving the room. As Roy had a room all to himself, she always made sure she switched off the light before closing the door, against his wish off course.

"Don't worry, there's nothing to be afraid of" was her usual phrase.

In less than thirty minutes, Roy had completely dozed off. A little after midnight, he suddenly woke up sweating profusely all over. He had just had a terrible nightmare. He dreamt a mysterious creature; probably some kind of spirit visited his room. The spirit was dressed as a clown and arrived in a colourful gliding sport car that fitted into the smallest and tiniest of holes. With a loud bang and a wave of the wand in his hand, the spirit transferred special powers into both of Roy's hands, and with another deafening bang, the spirit was gone. It was then Roy woke up.

The first thing he did was to gently pull up his blanket, so it could cover most of his face. He however left his eyes to peep round the room to ensure that everything was in its place, and that there wasn't another *thing* lurking nearby.

BANG!

Roy's sprit, soul and body almost parted ways in fright. On looking round the room though, he saw nothing. Or at least nothing that was not there before. He then looked out through the window and realized that all this while it had been raining. There were a lot of thunders and lightening which explained the loud bangs.

Roy wiped the sweat off his forehead with his right hand. He then tried to make himself more comfortable, so he could continue his sleep from where he left off. But he could not do so because no sooner had he closed his eye before he heard two people arguing. It was totally unlike his parents to argue aloud, and in any case, the voices he heard certainly belonged to neither of them. He did not expect Samson was talking to himself either and he was absolutely convinced it was not the T.V because it was always switched off before midnight.

Roy curved his left hands around his ear and turned it towards the direction the noise seemed to have been coming from. Something on his left hand brushed against his ear. It felt soft and somewhat...*alive*. Roy raised his left hand to see it properly from the little moonlight that was getting into his room. What he saw nearly made him lose his mind. His left hand had eyes, ears and a mouth of its own! Roy opened his mouth to scream but without his control, his right hand swung up and completely covered his mouth.

"Shut up! You are no longer a baby so what is scaring you stiff?" Roy could not believe his eyes. His left hand had just spoken to him in a very audible tone.

"Now back to where we stopped." Roy's right hand said. Roy noticed that his right hand also had its own pair of eyes, nose and a tiny mouth in the centre of its palm.

"By the way" His left hand started, "I'm Leslie"

"Leslie?" Roy asked utterly astonished. "Where on Earth did you get the name?!!" He had no idea his hands had names of their own.

"I gave myself the name of course! Or do you have a problem with that lil' boy?"

"No" Roy replied assertively. It was enough that every member of his family saw him as a baby. It could only be worse if his own hands had the same opinion.

"Good" Leslie said, "Now I won't have to smack you silly"

Turning to face Roy, his right hand spoke "Oh, just call me Right"

"Right???!" Leslie interrupted before Roy could make a statement.

"You see, that's the problem I have with you. You always think you are **right**. Somewhere in that little head of yours, you are the perfect one, the flawless soul, the strongest..."

"And who says I am not. You?" Right asked.

"Yes. ME, Leslie. You are nothing but a pain in the ass and an overenthusiastic labourer"

"What! How dare you?" Right said springing up from his position beside Roy. He toppled onto Leslie and tried to smother him. Roy was trying all he could, but he really could not do much.

Both hands seemed to have gotten a life and will of their own and he had little or no control over them.

"Will you two stop squabbling for one second and settle your differences like civilized people?!" Roy shouted, startling both hands that immediately let go of each other.

"Now, I want both of you to tell me what exactly the problem is"

"It's Right" Leslie was the first to speak. Turning suddenly to Roy, he pointed his index finger at him and added, "And of course, you."

"Both of you have conspired to make me look inferior."

"How" Roy asked.

"How? I'll tell you how. While you give Right the dignified jobs to do, you make me do all the dirty things like washing your smelling butt when you finish using the toilet."

"But...but" Roy stammered, "I really don't see the difference between what you do and what Right does."

"What do you mean you don't see the difference? Can you compare cleaning your butt or picking up dirty things to getting a warm handshake from Sandra?"

"Which Sandra?" Roy asked urgently

"How many Sandras seat beside you in class, Mr. Mama's boy?"

"Oh, that Sandra. Anyway, she's just a friend."

"Whatever" Right interjected after a long silence. "I see you find Caroline very pretty, Leslie" He said wriggling his wrist.

"It's a pity you'll never get to embrace lovely, lovely Caroline," He added, teasing Leslie.

"Hey, you guys are getting me confused here. I thought we were talking about Sandra just now. Who the hell then is Caroline? I sure don't know any Caroline in my...

"Do we have to spell it out to you all the time, Captain

Dumb?" Of the two hands, Leslie obviously had the sharpest and most insulting tongue.

"Caroline is Sandra's right hand, ok?"

"Geez! You mean, you mean Sandra's hands also have names of their own?" Roy asked again. Leslie simply hissed then continued his debate.

"Mind you, that's not all. Right also gets to convey food into your mouth, operate the remote control for the electronics, and receive gifts from your father."

"But all these are just due to tradition" Roy explained. "For instance, it will be wrong to receive gifts from my dad with my left hand, I mean you, Leslie."

"Tradition my foot"

"Like you have one" Right cut in. "In any case, you are simply jealous"

"Stop it. Don't say such mean things." Roy said

"As far as I am concerned, every single thing you get to do is more of a responsibility than a privilege. After all, it might as well have been the Leslie in your shoes and you in his. You were just lucky to be the right hand."

"Fancy you saying a thing like that" Leslie said, surprising Roy that he appeared to be defending Right.

"Does the name Richard ring a bell to you?" Leslie asked cunningly.

Roy thought for a second then realized what Leslie was trying to say. It just occurred to him that this situation was an exact replica of the scenario between him and Richard earlier in the day.

"Oh, I am so sorry. I promise to apologize to Richard first thing in the morning."

"Good" Right said with noncommittal.

"You guys seemed to have forgotten what we were taught at the last Sunday school in church. We read from...em..." "1 Corinthians 12:20 to the end." Leslie said and before anyone knew it, he started reciting the scripture verbatim.

"But now are there many members yet one body. And the eye cannot say unto the hand, I have no need of thee, or the head to the feet; I have no need of you. Nay much more those members of the body which seem to be feebler are necessary. And those members of the body, which we think to be less honourable, upon these we bestow more abundant honour and our uncomely (unattractive) parts have more abundant comeliness. For our comely parts have no need: but God hath tempered the body together, having given more abundant honour to that part which lacked. That there should be no Division in the body, but that members should have the same care for another. And..."

"Alright" Roy interrupted to prevent Leslie from reciting the

whole chapter.

"Leslie, I never knew you had such a good memory. Maybe you should be the one writing my tests for me." He said.

"C'mon Roy, I too could have easily recited those verses but...but" Right stuttered

"But what?" Leslie asked smiling.

"But for the fact that I had to flick through the Bible to locate the chapter and also trace the words with my finger as the teacher read it out"

"I expect you two to have learnt a lesson here. I myself never really understood that sermon until today. This all goes to say that both of you are equally important to me and the different functions you perform are equally necessary. For instance, if both you had to feed me, then who would give me water to drink?"

When Roy noticed that they still did not seem totally convinced, he added, "Right, can you remember the day dad's ceramic plate slipped from you?"

"Yes" Right answered soberly If it weren't for Leslie who caught it, it would have broken and then I would be very cross with you." Leslie's face lit up when Roy said this.

So, you see, there should be no more squabbling or comparisons among you because as far as I am concerned, you are both equal to me. Now hug yourselves to show me that you have resolved your differences." Leslie grabbed Right and gave him a long, warm hug. Few minutes later, and they had all slept off.

Roy woke up at 6.am when Samson came to his room. The first thing Roy said after greeting Samson was on the strange happenings of the night.

"Guess what, I had a long conversation with both of my hands last night while it was raining" Roy wished he hadn't just said what he did when he saw Samson's lips curling into a smile.

Now Samson had something to tease him with. Furthermore, he would use it as a proof to his dad that Roy was still the baby they had always known.

"First of all, not a single drop of water fell from the sky last night. Or does the sand outside look moist?" Roy blinked.

"Secondly," Samson's picked up Roy's hands and showed them one by one to him. "When did your hands develop mouths to talk to you?"

"You know what? I'll do you a favour. I won't mention this to anyone on the condition that you stop all this talk about you being grown up and," Samson handed Roy his towel and toothbrush. "Get ready for school. You are running late."

Roy was glad Samson hadn't laughed or ridiculed him.

However, he still believed every bit of what he saw and heard the previous night, dream or reality. He dashed into the bathroom.

Roy got to school before the blaring sirens were set off.

Luckily, he saw Richard immediately he entered the school compound. He ran up to him.

"Richard I will like to say I am sorry for all the wrong things I said and did to you. By the way," Roy dug his right hand into his pocket and brought out a printed letter and some money.

"Here's your excursion letter and some money from my dad. I asked him to give me money for an excursion to the zoo for my best friend in the whole wide world" Roy said smiling.

"Apology accepted" Richard said happily. I had a feeling God answered my prayer last night.

They both hugged themselves as a stunned Jane looked at them from the window of the classroom.

"Oh boy, how I thank God I don't have two right hands," Richard said as they walked hand in hand to their classroom. When he noticed Roy was staring at him with a puzzled expression, he looked back at Roy and winked.

7 DAYS

"There shall be five days of torture, and on the seventh day, a beast shall rise again"

"But...but, what then happens on the sixth day...today?" A question with such terrifying implications couldn't have been asked more simply.

"That's why we are here," The answer promised to be even simpler.

"To find out"

PROLOGUE

My heart pounded in a hundred thumps as I plunged blindly into the thick black forest in deep uncertainty. My five-foot physique got the trees thrusting hostile, sharp thorns in my face. As in a scornful hiss, the wind and the dry leaves conspired with my pursuer disclosing my locations. No one in my shoes will see such a hideous creature and challenge him to a duel. Hell no! Its charcoal black complexion and outstretched two-edged claws depicted a horrid picture from hell. A long, slender eye on its forehead easily earned it the name Cyclops, but another minute eye on its bare belly changed all that.

"⌁⑨⑨✎✎𝒆𝒓⑥❶⑥ଢ③❺ଯ☙❀①⑤ᖭ" It murmured in a strange language impossible to represent in written form. The wide chase continued, forcing me deeper and deeper into the forest. *Is this just a terrible nightmare, or is it true?* I asked myself praying the former was the case.

I could remember the stories Yolly, an ex-student had told me about cannibals in the school forest.

Then I had laughed at him. He spoke of half men-half horses and talking trees among other tales I had tagged as 'Yolly's lullabies' He had even shown a mild indignation when he sensed that his stories did not move me to fear.

●①⑤⑤☙⑨▤ ☙①⑤⑤☙⑨✎ A voice like roaring thunder a few inches behind me reminded me of my present predicament.

That was when I saw it.

A streak of God-sent light sparked some fire in my eyes. Perhaps, I would still live a little bit longer. Maybe I still have a chance with that pretty girl in my class. All I had to do was dash through...

"Aaa!" I was presently hoping, or better still praying I'd land in my mother's hands or at least in school, but of course that was a fantasy.

While running, the creeping roots of a tree got entangled with my legs, hence my sudden flight.

I landed with a great thump on my right elbow but that didn't matter a bit. At least, not until I realized that standing up seemed a bit difficult, a little Herculean, convincingly impossible. I caught sight of a small girl in the school pinafore a few feet from my burial ground. She was last month reported as 'strangely dead' Rumours held that she committed suicide due to family problems she considered herself responsible for. It was now obvious that was a great deviation from the truth. Perhaps the same will be said about me. In my case, that the suicide was because of my inability to express my childish feelings to the person I dreamt of every night. Who said children don't fall in love?

He or rather, it, was now towering over me, certainly ready for dinner...ೲ①⑤⑤ೱ⑨

I could see the headlines in 'The Daily Sun' November 22nd 1999.

"J.S.S 2 boy of F.G.C.L dies under mysterious circumstances." I shut my eyes in an attempt to say a last prayer, but instead just waited for my imminent division. The creature was unmistakably hungry judging by the drops of hot saliva that fell on my head. It lowered its trunk, gently. It smelt of death and I realized I was its prey as it revealed a pair of long fangs never seen in any vampire movie. It was breathing hot air on my neck, which ironically, was really chilling.

It then got closer, and closer...

16th November 1999

66 Hallelujah! We are back in school. Thank God; no more 'silly chores' Rakim said as he placed his mattress on his bed.

"That's what he'll say now. In two weeks' time, he'll be crying every night and writing letters every morning to his mum, "I miss you, I miss you…" Just at that instance, Jide Famakin walked abruptly into the room with only a polythene nylon bag. "Eyin boys, the fine boy of this room is back from his mid-term break o! So come and welcome me" Jide was again brushing his meticulously brushed hair as he said this.

"Na your type" I cut in for the second time. "Abeg, shut up" Jide got indignant. "What do you know about fine?" he asked. "Just one thing" I said, "That you are far from it"

"Shit!" Isioma who had been silently observing the scenario felt it was high time he also talked. "Tayo, you did not finish with Rakim, yet you've already gone to someone else"

"Tayo, shey? He likes *yabbing* people" That was Ifeanyin talking. He was the god's gift to the Igbo people. He ate in Igbo, read English with an intense Igbo accent and even dreamt aloud in Igbo.

"Don't let me start with you" I retaliated. "Please don't, I know you will finish me in no time at all." Ifeanyin pleaded jokingly. Anyway, I had already started in my mind. Do you think we are snoring in Igbo here?

Hey! Do not get me wrong, it's not like I am nasty or a troublesome fellow, because as a matter of fact, I am neither. It is just that *yabbing* people was what I did for fun, and I guess my roommates understood that fact because right now, everyone in the room were laughing hysterically.

I carefully counted for the umpteenth time the money my dad gave me- ten twenty Naira notes and two fifty Naira notes. I made a mental note to transfer the money to my metallic box when the lights were put out for the day.

"Haba, Tayo, why are you removing your trousers? Who told you I haven't seen your dead boxer shorts already? By the way, have you..." That was Alatise, my next bunk neighbour rambling.

I did not bother answering any of his questions. I placed all the money in the right pockets of my boxers. Keeping it in the pockets of my trousers would mean I did not want it at all. Seniors would come down on it like vultures on a carcass.

"Tayo, why don't you ever answer my questions?"

How would I when you ask so many silly ones?

"O, I know what you are thinking." Alatise said. "You think I ask too many questions, or is it too many silly questions?" He just couldn't help himself.

When we were in our first year in this school, he asked if we would still live with our parents by the time we were in our final year, S.S.3. C'mon, to him the S.S.3 boys seemed so old; they could as well have their own kids to cater for by then.

"By the way, what about the spoon of Bournvita I lent you last term, you promised to refund it, remember?"

Victor would you please just shut up?

"Hey!" I almost screamed my head off. "Would you please just shut up for one microsecond? I'm trying to think here"

"Think about?"

"V.A for stupid" Jide knew just when to get involved. He had this third eye that made him know when an argument was in the making. I looked at my CAT wristwatch to know the time-3 p.m. Victor was lying on his bed. His eyes were wide open and he was staring at the bed above his. A quick glance at my left hand and with a parting of his lips, I know what he wanted to say.

Is that a wristwatch you are wearing?

Being the smart boy that he was, he refrained. "Don't worry; no more questions from my side." "That is why I like you. You are intelligent" I meant every word I had just said. Victor was what you would call a boy genius. He had entered Secondary School at the age of nine. Out of the seventeen subjects we offered in our first JSS 1, he got a whooping sixteen distinctions, way ahead the nine distinctions many other students found hard to exceed.

"Let us take a stroll to the class area"

The surprise in Victor's eyes was evident. I guess that was why he never got tired of asking me questions. Many other boys who had ever been in his corner (bed area) always vacated it after two weeks because of his childishness. Not me. One minute, I was boiling and the next minute, we were playing a game together.

Through the open door, I saw Ifeanyi coming towards my room. His checked short sleeved shirt, the compulsory dormitory wear, was not tucked in. He seemed to be singing. **Singing?** "Uhh!"

"I snogged a bloke once but it didn't float my boat" Ifeanyi sang with a voice very similar to that of Obasanjo's.

"I can bet on my life that you don't know who sang that song" Naturally, that was Jide.

Victor and I instinctively cut our journey short. We could see it coming. Nonetheless, Ifeanyi headed back to where he had just come from. *'Let sleeping dogs lie'* I thought. However, Jide was not the type to give up the chance to start a fight. He shouted at Ifeanyi's back. "It was Robbie Williams, you *Igbotic* freak"

Ifeanyi looked back

The whole room started paving way for a wrestling match, our favourite pastime. Bunks were shifted to the wall and sharp objects were concealed. As cruel as our encouraging fights may seem, we always tried to keep casualties at a minimal level. Unfortunately for the commentators who had taken places at opposite ends of the room, Ifeanyi just walked across the quadrangle that separated the two rows of rooms that made up the dormitory, back to his room. After lots of hisses and sighs, one of the commentators deemed it fit to think straight.

"I pity you, Jide, u think say na by height?"

"Okay, so na by wetin?" Jide threw the question back to Rakim.

"Strength"

The whole room suddenly went so silent, we could hear our neighbouring rats deliberate on strategies for the night, solar eclipses were not as rare as hearing Victor on the answering side of a question.

He was right nevertheless. While Jide was the tallest boy in the room, Ifeanyi was the oldest and about the strongest boy in the entire dormitory! As far as the physical was concerned, Jide was no match for Ifeanyi.

"Don't let me lose my temper" A usually quiet Teju was the one talking.

"What??!" Jide hoped Teju was challenging him to a duel. Teju once reported Jide to a teacher for cheating in a class test, and Jide had been silently, but fervently praying for the opportunity to make Teju feel the pain he felt when he got thwacked.

"Don't get agitated, that's what Ifeanyi murmured when he entered the room and I was of the opinion that maybe...you should know.

So you mean you walked all the way from room 7 to room 3 to 'do gbegborun'?

I did not bother asking him anyway because I knew what his answer would be; *Tayo, don't let the devil and his legions of demons use you o!*

Teju was of average height with a moderately stout body. Many people kept away from him because he was some sort of religious fanatic and also what we call a *'kasali'*- someone who was always out to please his teachers, seniors and any other person he felt was in charge. His roommates were always the first to wake up in the morning. This was because once Teju started binding and loosening spiritual strongholds at 4.30 in the morning, no eye could stay shut. Anyone who dared to criticize his prayer bouts became a major prayer point for the next morning:

"Lord, don't let ... be used by the devil, Lucifer, prince of darkness and of this world...to inhibit your work here in this dormitory and school. Fire!! Fire!!..."

So you see; everyone just let him be.

"Are you no longer coming along with me?" Victor asked me.

"Why not? Let's be on our way, now that Ifeanyi has disappointed us."

A few steps and we were out of the dormitory. Like every other dormitory in the boarding area, ours consisted of eight rooms. Six of the rooms each contained students that belonged to a particular house, while the other two had a mixture of different houses. The houses in questions were groups to which students belonged. Each house wore a unique colour of checked clothing. I belonged to Jaja House and we were housed in room 3. Room one belonged to Dan Fodio (green), Room two, El Kanemi (brown), Room five Macauly (Purple), six, Moremi (yellow), and seven, Oduduwa (red). Rooms four and eight were the mixed rooms. The houses were named after dead Nigerian heroes.

"Jaja!!" Melo called from a distance with a flick of his forefinger. Victor and I immediately knew he was calling us.

"Wetin una get for your pockets" Two peculiar characteristics about most of our seniors were: 1. Most of them never spoke pure English.

2. The majority of them never seemed to have real names. We only knew their nicknames.

"Wey my BBD?" A fierce looking Mc Don by his side also asked when we refused to answer. BBD was acronym for big boys due. A so-called big boy was the elite, the one with the money and girls. Yeah, right. I didn't fit that profile, but who cared? Certainly not these scavengers.

Method, who had only been staring at Victor's pockets all this while grabbed him and began searching vigorously like they do at the airports for hard drugs.

Every single kobo was extracted from Victor; about three hundred Naira in all. Melo who had just finished applying the same technique with me found nothing, thanks to my boxers.

"The J.Bs (junior boys) of these days are fucking poor" He spat as he said this. *What an Irony.* I thought.

"This boy, wey my *sheddars*?" Mc don was waving his right hand at me as he said this.

Did you give me money to keep for you?

I dared not say that though, else I would be mincemeat.

"I said, where is my *doe*, or have you suddenly gone deaf?"

Mc don must have been really dumb to think, that me, Tayo Adelabi, was going to be intimidated to give him a penny from the money chilling in the right pocket of my boxers. Not even a Mike Tyson punch would do that right now.

I feigned a pleading sound and was about to deliver my usual story of how my mum was in a coma, and my dad had gone hopelessly broke and jobless.

"Run away *jo!*" Melo shouted at me. "That guy na stingy bastard"

The last thing I cared about right now was the language with which they used to describe me. After all, the use of vulgar languages appeared to grow with each class succumbed in this school. The only thing that really mattered right now was the crispy Naira notes in my pocket crying to be spent.

"Those guys are surfs" Victor had recovered from the shock of losing his money and was now ready to talk. He was in tears as he said those words.

"Are your parents coming to see you next week" Hey, help me out here, as sure as I knew what my name is, I knew the answer to that question was a definite yes, but I was only trying to be sympathetic here, you know, sensitive.

"Yes" He said, noncommittally.

"Those useless made men guys are bloody surfs" A 'Surf' was the shortened form of sufferer. Surfs are people who are abjectly poor, miserable, and pitiable. If I had infrared vision, I would have seen the venom coming out of my friend's mouth.

"I guess I'll rather call them made monkeys" I added again, even more sympathetically.

S.S 3 boys had formed several clicks among themselves. There were the "Made Men", who had just exploited us, the "Wutang clan", named after a rap group in the U.S, and the "No Limit crew", also with affiliations with a rap group. A good number of them dressed in similar fashions, and some even went as far as making customized T-shirts for themselves. They were the equivalent of the so-called clubs of universities.

"I wonder if our mates will be like that in the future," I thought aloud.

"God forbid"

"What makes you so sure?" I asked him.

"Well, I can't say *sha*, but I am sure that I wouldn't be like that. My mummy..."

My sudden laughter cut short Victor's mummy story short.

"So what's so funny?" He obviously thought I was ridiculing him.

He followed my eyes as they set on Mr. Odebayo and his daughter.

"What's so hilarious about a man holding his daughter?" He probably thought I was lying about what it was that was amusing me.

I remember when one of our mates asked her, "How do you do?"

"Guess what she said?"

"What?" Victor was already laughing.

"I do fine" I said, then joint in the laughter.

"You know, you really can't blame her, her dad is only a security man."

"I doubt that counts," I said, defending my point. "After all, she goes to school." Anyway, some of our mates aren't any better, they still *shell* like hell"

"Like who?" I asked him.

"Isioma"

"Isioma who?"

"Isioma Iwat" He answered quickly as his eyes began twitching when he saw his senior sister talking intimately with one of our mates in front of the gate that led into the girl's compound.

I ignored his sudden reaction and said, "Isioma's is a special case. He needs deliverance"

****

Beautiful. I thought as Foluke walked towards my direction. Her hair was cut low and uncombed; her skirt was way beyond her knees, her face was pimples ridden and her breath usually smelt like hell... Okay, I admit, I have no idea what hell smells like. It is just that it smelt so terrible I got the feeling hell had to smell like it, or at least something really close.

Basically, it wasn't her I felt was beautiful. It was the stuff in her hands.

"*Omo*, this guy, you are lucky o!" Oyetunji, who happened to be sitting right beside me on the dining hall bench said. He was seriously salivating.

"Haba, Oyetunji, you like food too much. Now, now, you've already become Tayo's best friend."

"Thomas shut up and stop acting like you won't also beg." Oyetunji snapped back. "Besides, I was only asking him how come they were related"

"I looked at my wrist. The time was 7.30 p.m."

"So Tayo, how did you two know each other?" He said aloud before whispering in my ears. "Abeg, I dey o! I never *chop* since morning"

I smiled my okay to him, and then answered his question nevertheless.

"She is the first daughter of my dad's colleague, who coincidentally...em...is a cousin to my dad's uncle's mother"

Although Oyetunji was certainly not concerned whether I had just read all I said from a storybook, he looked puzzled. His brains were definitely not up to the task.

"I'm confused" He managed to blurt out. "Me too" I said sincerely.

"Thanks" I told Foluke who had just dropped a pot of fish and stew on my table.

"If you like, continue to act like a big boy and don't eat. You hear?" Was all she said.

"Thanks" I said again.

Barely a second after she turned her back, Thomas and Oyetunji among many other boys had abandoned the food on their table and were almost suffocating me with their clattering steel plates.

"Alright, alright. One by one." I begged them.

Lying on my Mouka mattress, I rubbed my stomach carefully then looked at my watch- it read, nine hours, twenty-two minutes and fifty-six seconds. I had a habit of staring at my wristwatches for the first three weeks after buying them. After that time, they either got stolen, spoilt, or I just lost interest in them.

"Thanks once more for dinner" Bode said gently as he passed by.

"It was nothing," I said.

Bode is the most intelligent and best-behaved boy in my class. He was about the only person in this school of two thousand pupils who I was yet to insult directly or in my thoughts. Believe me- that was rare. He is what you may call a semi-angel. He didn't even stamp his foot when he walked, and I guess it was because he was afraid of hurting some crawling thing in the process.

Someone was banging the poles on the corridors of the dormitory.

"Come out for assembly! Come out for assembly!"

I did not have to strain my ear before I heard Teju's voice.

"Assembly time. Everybody come out."

I rushed out like a mad bull. I had no intention whatsoever to be the dorm prefect's first scapegoat of the rest of the term. We all assembled in straight lines, room by room, and then maintained absolute silence.

"Hey, I'm not the one calling assembly. I just want to tell you guys something. Do you wanna hear me? Ugo asked

"Yes!" We all echoed. It was funny he was asking whether or not we wanted to hear him out like we had a choice.

Ugo was in S.S.2 He repeated in his first year at the senior secondary school because of alleged health problems, which I sincerely doubted was the reason for his failure. He called himself...

"I'm don Makawiya; I ask why when other people die, because if I try, they will just cry"

Right now, I felt like doing exactly what he said people did when he tried. Like crazy, I wanted to cry because though stoning was a much more rational option, I was compelled like the rest of my mates to laugh. Don Makawiya was visibly elated. He believed he was the tightest emcee to walk the untarred roads of this college and was certain we hadn't seen anyone as funny as him. If only he knew...

"In your mind now, you don crack" 'His majesty', Joseph Samuels had just walked out after keeping us waiting for ten minutes, and like that wasn't enough, he had left us with sand flies and don Makawiya. Some people were just naturally mean. I hissed (In my mind, of course.)

Ugo looked at Joseph in disgust, and then fought back. "Which kind *mis-yarning* be that?" It was a sort of legal code that you never embarrassed your mates in front of juniors.

"You no even get sense of humour anyway, you bloody demon" Ugo said, as he walked out of the dormitory, boiling with fury. Very gently, I nodded my agreement with what Ugo said about Joseph being a demon.

Joseph was not in the least fazed. He just hissed, then wasted the next ninety minutes saying nonsense I didn't consider paying serious attention to.

17th November 1999

What I hated most about the mornings after resumptions was the manner in which we were woken up. At home, I usually slept till I was sick of sleeping, so it was terribly frustrating to suddenly hear a blaring siren or metal poles being banged like someone was on fire. People who refused to wake up were flogged out of their beds by the dormitory prefect. From what I had seen of Joseph, he had seriously mastered the use of the wooden poles that he used to flog us on our beds when we refused to listen to the banging poles- believe me, I've tasted it several times.

I woke up with a fright, sweating all over. My left hand dashed into my pillowcase to bring out my bunch of keys while my right hand simultaneously dragged my by box from under my bed. In less than three seconds, the top of my box fled open. My hands moved as quickly as Marion Jones' legs, and as smoothly as Ben Carson's hands to the top right-hand corner of my box, then began digging vigorously beneath my folded house wears.

Geez, thank God

I heaved a sigh of relief on touching my wallet. But somehow, I wasn't totally satisfied. I brought out all the money inside and counted every note- Three hundred Naira in all. Complete.

"What's up? Why are you sweating like that? Was any of your stuff stolen?"

I did not care if Victor asked a thousand and one questions. The important thing was that all my money was safe. Last night, someone's hands searched my pockets, probably for my key or some money. I was so scared stiff, I couldn't move a muscle. What if it was a spirit? What if the person had a weapon in his hands? In retrospect, it's funny how all those irrational questions got into my mind. I mean, who really believes in ghosts?

I stood up to go brush my teeth then I thought of Victor's last question. My spinal cord could have easily gotten damaged because of the speed with which I used to look at the back of my bunk-the exact position where I hung my scrupulously smoothened school uniform the night before. It had vanished- Disappeared into thin air. Vaporized!

"Someone has cleared your uniform, abi? Do you have a second one?"

"Yes" I quickly answered, before he concurrently asked eight other questions. "But it is rough. It is folded in my box."

"Man, it is bad for your uniform to be rough on the first day after resumption"

I wished he hadn't reminded me.

In less than eighty minutes, Victor, Bode and I were waiting in front of the dining hall gate. It was Monday morning, and hence, synonymous to a breakfast of bread and tea.

Oshame, one of the dining hall prefects stood protectively in front of the gate. He was a very stout boy with a receding hairline. One of his colleagues came to whisper something in his ear. He suddenly looked at us and then said, in a matter-of-fact manner, "No more bread. Go to your classes" That was it. No food that morning. It was finished, and no one gave a damn if we paid a million box for feeding, the food was just...finished.

"I don't know why, anytime that bastard is in front of the gate, I never get food to eat" Victor could be very vulgar when he was hungry.

"After waiting and lining up for... In short, let's go to the..." I on the other hand never completed my sentences when I was hungry.

"It is a pity he repeated. I learnt he was quite intelligent before." So you see; Bode was really the totally different one. If he got slapped in the face, he first worried about the person who slapped him. H made sure the person's fingers weren't hurting him, he begged for forgiveness even when he was right, then walked away without hissing in the least.

"I don't know why you pity him. This boy, you are somehow *sef*. After all, it was because he wanted to become a prefect that he repeated on purpose."

"And what makes you think so" Bode asked very gently. Victor got angry, hissed and walked away. Very few boys could put up with Bode's don't-hurt-anyone attitude. I barely managed myself because it was often confusing whether it was saintly, or out rightly stupid. Well, be the judge.

Every single class in the school consisted of eight arms- F, G, C, J, L, N, U and S. They represented the full name of the school- Federal Government College Ijanikin, Lagos, Nigeria Unity School. I was in J.S.S 2 L. As in my earlier year, I sat in the front, at the far-left corner of the class. I loved the seat because it was near the window, so when the teacher got really boring, I took solace in looking outside the window. The seat also afforded me the opportunity to lean back and observe everybody else in the class when there was no teacher around. Today was one of such moments.

"Ehen, If you see how Baba Suwe was doing his mouth in the movie, *A o logbon...*"Bisi was nodding her pretty head, and probably thinking of a way to escape from the conversation with Sade. It is not like I was exactly eavesdropping on their conversation, it is just that when Sade whispered, the whole class heard; and when she spoke normally, the whole block heard her. Sade White was just a bit shorter than me. The hairstyles she wore made her look 200 years older. Worse still, she was not good in the looks department either. Our mathematics' teacher advised her to join the debating society because she could not keep her lips together, but she refused. Being useful contravened everything she stood for.

Mr. Olawunmi walked into the class. As usual, he had his green Kaftan on, with black leather slippers supposedly made by Versace on his feet. The spot just below the embroidery on his cloth had a tiny hole about two millimetres long. The hem of his trousers had gotten weak from too much washing, and as at the last count, it had been loosened twice. If I was a good artist, I would be able to sketch Mr. Olawunmi, the physical health education teacher in pitch darkness.

"We don't have P.H.E now!" Many girls protested. The man paused, squinted his eyes, and then asked, "Are you sure?" in his usual drunken way.

"Yes sir!" The whole class echoed assertively.

"But it is not possible to have the entrance of Port Harcourt here. You do not understand, it is a very big city..." The dumb students in the class, mostly the girls laughed, while the boys booed him. His dry sense of humor coupled with his unyielding character was something that put most boys off. In J.S.S. 1, he happened to be our housemaster. He enacted several silly laws, one of which was that we should pour drained water from *garri* through the window each time our seniors came to extort money or provisions from us. We were still suffering the consequences of our actions, as most of the seniors affected had become our sworn enemies and were eager to let us know at the slightest provocation. Now that we were no longer the babies of the principal, we were simply tender lambs placed in the care of fierce looking, hungry wolves.

All the man came to do was to call his ward, Emmanuel, but that appeared to be taking forever because of his talkativeness. He was presently talking to the assistant class captain. I call her 1st class Dundee. Silly Yoruba words like 'shoo', 'boo', 'gbo', and 'iro' amused her. On the other hand, simple topics like arithmetic, transitive verbs and prepositions totally threw her off balanced. It was like explaining the coordinates of a satellite to a two-year-old infant.

"See your hair like banana"

She laughed

"It looks like your teeth"

She laughed again

"Don't look at me jo'. I am not your husband"

She laughed yet again!

"Uhh!" I said, holding my stomach. "Isn't that girl dumb?"

But of course, Bode, sitting by my side never answered questions like that. To him, they were inappropriate, uncalled for, really mean, not thoughtful...

"Have you done your math assignment?"

"Which one?" I asked, suddenly tense.

"Don't tell me that you've forgotten about it. She gave us as our midterm homework"

"Oops! I had totally forgotten about it." Perspiration began forming on my forehead as the face of the 'she' in question began forming before my terrified eyes. "So when is she collecting it?" I asked again. He looked at my wristwatch to my utmost delight then replied: "Em... in about 15 minutes time."

"Ye!" I exclaimed as I dug into my locker to look for my notebook.

****

Piles of faeces of different colours lay everywhere on the floor- brown, black and green. A particular lump looked somewhat bluish or maybe it was just my eyes.

I tiptoed carefully to avoid stepping on any of the piles till I got to a moderately clean toilet. I again exhaled gently to avoid upsetting the pack of flies that had taken over the entire toilet. I then opened my fly to release 'junior.' My right hand went in carefully; I did not want to scare him.

Somehow, it was not there. ***No, this ain't right.*** I poked my left had also in case my right hand's reach was somehow short, still no answer. I felt like screaming, but if I did, I would be viciously attacked by the flies for disturbing their peace. Strangely, prior to coming to the toilet, the ever-superstitious Ifeanyi mentioned that in his village no one allowed old women to tap them on the back.

He cited an example of a small boy who lost his penis after such an incident. They tried tracing the old woman only to find out that she had already travelled to faraway Cotonou to meet her booty.

God forbid! I have a whole generation of chicks to cater for.

Then I found it. It had shrunk, probably due to the cold, and was crumpled in a tiny corner in between my legs. I had just saved myself from embarrassing Sade who mistakenly hit me when I was coming out of the dining hall.

"When I finished using the toilet, I remembered a popular phrase from our J.S.S 1: '*Tinuke shit, toilet fall*'

Tinuke was an albino who weighed about a 100 kg at that time. It was rumoured that the very first day she set her butt on the W.C, there was disaster. The toilet scattered into several tiny pieces. Students and teachers alike taunted her all the time over the incident till she got fed up and left the school for good.

I went to my room to pack the clothes I wanted to wash. I was billed to provide detergents and buckets while my roommate, Seun, fetched the water- it was what we called a corporative, use what you have to get what you want.

I was still waiting in the quadrangle for Seun to begin washing when Chike walked into the dormitory. Chike a.k.a Reverendevil was the most notorious student to have worn the uniform of this school till date. He was about six feet tall and heavily built. He was presently walking towards me as if tele-guided by some sort of spirit. My knees wobbled. I had absolutely no idea that something was about to change forever- my life, or else I would have done something drastic. Disappeared...covered myself in sand...or at least something a bit more realistic, but definitely drastic, like drinking some of the soapy water.

"Wash these clothes" He said and started walking away before I could think of a reasonable excuse why I couldn't wash his clothes. Reverendevil's clothes. Should I say I was asthmatic? Ironically the guy washing behind us was a confirmed asthmatic patient and even had an attack yesterday. What about the pain in my right hand at the spot where our math teacher had flogged me hungrily? Would that be a good enough excuse? Somehow, I doubted it. Okay, maybe claiming to have typhoid would make more sense. Wasn't it said that typhoid was a water- borne disease? And is it not water that was used to wash clothes? But I wasn't even convinced myself. Since I could not find anything meaningful to say, all that escaped my lips was: "But...I...I..."

He stopped, turned back and started walking quickly towards me. **He had a cold stare in his eyes.** The same he had when he hit an S.S.1 boy's head against the wall three times...**His hands had formed into a fist-** The same way it was before he plucked out the teeth of his mate who refused to give him a packet of biscuit.

He was just an arm's length from me.

"But what?" He asked in a deep voice that echoed through every fibre of my being

"But...but...when...where should I keep it...em..." My words stumbled on each other like a pack of old cards.

He must have noticed how seriously I was sweating and shaking because he simply turned back and continued his walk out of the dormitory.

"I'll come back for it," He said. I heaved a heavy sigh of relief that he said 'it' and not 'you'.

That would have left me with no other choice but to write a suicide note.

By now, Seun was ready with the water. "What's up?" he asked after he made sure that Chike was about two thousand feet away from the dormitory.

"He asked me to wash his clothes." I replied grudgingly. "It is just that I'm pitying him, if not I could have easily decided not to wash them. After all, will he kill me?"

"Stop deceiving yourself. You know very well that you can't do that"

Need I say that Seun was right?

We washed our shirts first, followed by underwear, then finally, pairs of trousers and socks.

Although I left my clothes outside to dry, I dared not try that with a senior's clothes, a devilish one for that matter. This was because in this dormitory, a lot of things simply disappeared. So I hung the clothes on the broken ceiling sheets in my room, dragged a locker to that spot and got ready to sit down for hours.

I had barely stayed there for thirty minutes when Isioma came whistling past me holding a wooden board in his hands. The board was used by the introductory technology students for technical drawing. For guys like Isioma though, the board had an entirely different use.

"Shey u go play Ijanikin soccer?"

One other thing about Isioma was that till date, I have never heard him speak any other language apart from Pidgin English.

"Nah" I answered waving my right hand. "I'm watching over Chike's *baffs*, abeg, I don't want *gbese*" Isioma looked up at where my finger was pointing but still did not give up.

"No fear, we go dey that corner," He said, pointing at Seun's bed area, about five steps away from the centre of the room where the clothes were hanging. To convince me further, he added, "U go fit watch the baffs from there"

Inasmuch as I disliked Isioma Iwat's playfulness, he knew how to get me to relax.

"Get ready for some serious thrashing" I said, jumping off the locker.

Ijanikin soccer was played using a padlock and a button. Holes on opposite ends of the board were used as goalposts, while the button was the ball. The padlock is then spun in a clockwise direction and the person to play tried to manoeuvre the board to make the spinning padlock hit the button into the opponent's post. When the padlock stopped spinning, it was the turn of the other guy to play. Like I earlier implied, by the time three minutes had elapsed, I was leading Isioma by six goals to nil.

As a matter of fact, I was still jubilant over my seventh goal when I heard the most important question Victor had ever asked before.

"Tayo, you've packed Chike's clothes, right?"

I twisted my entire torso so I could have a really good look before calling him a questionnaire.

"Geez!"

"Do you guys know what?" None of us knew what answer to give Joseph.

"Una dey craze. Can't you answer a simple question?" About a hundred or so nervous voices murmured, "We can!"

"Alright, I'll ask my question again". By now Joseph was loosening his belt. I hoped it was because he wanted some fresh air.

"Wetin una do?" He asked again, his eyes red with hatred. The veins on his square forehead popped with indignation in synchrony with the muscles in his arms. Still that was not enough to make all of us think alike and say the same thing like universal soldiers. So everybody just said something in a bid to avoid what, unfortunately, was already happening.

Joseph had jumped into the quadrangle and was swinging his metal studded leather belt everywhere he could.

"If you dare move eh..." His chest heaved up and down very rapidly.

"...I would kill you!" From every corner of the quadrangle were 'yees' and 'ahhs' as the metal stud at the edge of the belt tattooed Joseph's trademarks on the body of my mates. Luckily for me, I was standing closely behind Joseph, so I did not feel very serious pain.

"In just two days, eh?" Joseph who had climbed the corridor to talk like a normal human being again jumped onto the quadrangle to increase the yelling.

"You guys have defecated everywhere in the toilets. There is even no way to pa...pass again."

His arms swung yet again.

"In short, take the first position of Mario world"

Hey! I was also a victim of this toilet mishap. I shouldn't be punished along with the others.

At times like this, I wished I were the boldest man on Earth, so I could say just what I felt.

Mario world was a series of punishments consisting of eight stages; each stage lasted for about three minutes. Till date, no group of people had exceeded the fifth stage because someone was always likely to faint at the fourth. First, you lay flat on your belly, breathing into the sand. At the next stage, you rested your entire weight on your elbows and toes. This punishment was popularly called 'Agama', probably named after the famous agama lizard. It was at this stage that Joseph's poles always came in handy as he flogged anyone who was not serving the punishment correctly. The third stage, though an easier task was not any better due to the accumulated pain of the first two stages. We were to kneel and raise our hands, simultaneously waving our fingers.

By now, about seventy percent of the dormitory was crying and moaning with the most sorrowful sounds they could produce.

Joseph was still contemplating if we should move on to the angle ninety stage when a heavily built body bearing a familiar face entered the dormitory unnoticed, the way a lion would when it was going for the kill.

I was surprised I hadn't gotten brain haemorrhage or some dangerous mental breakdown yet because my heart had just skipped ten beats at the sight of this deadly creature...Chike!

"Who be Tayo for this place." That deep voice made me say the quickest prayers ever muttered as I literally crawled to meet Devil's number one hit man.

18th November

"Abeg, did you help me see the baffs I hung in the centre of the room?" Those were the first words that came out of my mouth when someone woke me up.

"I pity you. Do you know the time? Or is it that you want Joseph to flog you again this morning before you take your bath?

I'm not sure if it was Victor's questions that irritated me or maybe it just dawned on me that everybody in the room already had on their school uniforms. I grabbed the red plastic bucket Victor's hand held out to me and sprinted out of the room. It was musty and cold outside, but I didn't even give it a second thought. I almost toppled on my mate as I pushed my bucket under the tap.

"Wetin dey do you now? The boy asked. "Sorry" I managed to blurt out.

Although my entire body was aching from last night's ordeal, I carried the bucket of water like it was an accident victim being rushed to the emergence room.

Heaven knows how many people I shoved aside and how many more cursed me in return as I rushed to my room. At the room, Victor did not forget to remind me of the time.

"Do you know it is 6. 40a.m already?" And as if that was not enough, he had also taken the pains to calculate how many more minutes I had before we were ordered out of the dormitory.

"Shey you haven't forgotten that Joseph will pursue us out of the dormitory by 6.45 a.m?" The combinations of words like ordered, pursue and JOSEPH always sent a chill down my spine. I peeled off my polka dotted pyjamas, picked up my soap case and dashed out of the room. I did not bother to listen to Victor's narration of what Joseph usually did to people found in the bathroom when it was time to 'run out of the dormitory'. If forfeiting taking my bath was what Victor was proposing, then he had gotten it all wrong. That was not just an alternative. Yesterday, I managed to get Bisi to look in my direction by the perfume I put on (don't bother wondering if I borrowed it). I was not about to jeopardize that success because of one lousy human being- Yes! Not even Chike. It was the pangs of pain in my body that had prevented me from hearing

Joseph when he came to our room to announce that he was not going to wake anybody up today, but that anyone who was caught in the bathroom when it was time to leave the dormitory will...

The guy bathing by my side also mentioned that Joseph did not finish the sentence as he dashed out of the bathroom and wished me good luck

"One...two...three" My heart raced in symphony with the counted numbers. There was however soap in my eyes so the possibility of running out of the bathroom was reduced. In any case, nobody did, because the only guy who attempted to run out of the bathroom first got slapped before he was pushed back inside.

I was lucky not to have seen the smile Joseph had on his lips as he locked us in the bathroom or else it would hunt me forever. It was then that I realized how truthful Makawiya had being when he called Joseph a bloody demon.

An hour elapsed before Joseph came to open the gate. By this time, every other person had gone to the dining hall. Hence, we had missed our breakfast. I made a mental calculation of how much money I had left with me. In J.S.S.1, I spent so much money in my first week in school that I was writing home in no time at all. Trust my people, there was no response till the final visiting day before the mid-term break by which time I had adapted to the broke status by falling in love with the dining hall.

Each of us in the bathroom had dressed up by begging our 'free' friends to get our clothes for us. Victor helped me with mine when he came on one of his several detective missions to the bathroom to ask me if I knew what I was about to witness.

"How many are you guys?" Our dormitory prefect asked. We counted ourselves smartly. "Twelve" The boy who had tried to escape had taken the leadership position. One thing that impressed me about my mates was how quickly we were able to organize ourselves when we were about to be beaten or punished.

"Every fuck up must be treated" Something about the intonation in Joseph's voice, reminded me why I had never gone to church. Joseph was one of the officials in the church and actually led the prayer and praise section. He was the reason why on Sundays, rather than go to church, I read a portion of the Bible then played ball or read my books.

You guys should come out in a file and hold the poles, one person to each pole. Joseph tried to frighten us by talking in whispers. To say how annoying that was would be an understatement, I was furious. What the hell did he take us for? Typical Joseph. He loved it when junior students were begging him with all they had, knowing that would not change anything. *So does he think he is so scary? In short, I wouldn't move when he flogs me.* I thought.

"Shey when I was talking the other night, you all thought I was saying nonsense." It was at this same instance that my palms settled on the long cold steel poles so it was no surprise that immediately, my mouths turned sour. All the guts I had just tried building up instantly vanished.

"Monkeys!" Joseph spat out as he removed the nails from one of the several wooden net-poles he was about to break on our backs. "Thank God I did not sleep on a top bunk or is this how this guy would have wasted my net pole?". I thought out loud, trying to console myself by taking my mind off what I was about to witness. That however did not work especially when Tolu who was beside me hissed after he heard what I said. "This guy, it is like you don't know what's up" He had said, sweat dripping off his face. I was not surprised though, because he was Joseph's customer. He had this flare for getting into trouble. It was either today he did not do his work portion, or tomorrow, his bed was not laid with white bed sheets.

By now, Joseph had started flogging Peter. Peter was one of the most hardened boys in our set so when I heard him scream in pain with each stroke, my legs turned jelly.

I was the eighth person on the line so it seemed like forever before it was my turn to get flogged. The reality struck me when I looked directly into Joseph's unsmiling face. It was my turn to be judged! Damn! I wished for an earthquake, earth tremor, volcano-Anything at all to prevent Joseph's pole from hitting me.

"Are you crazy? Didn't you hear when I said you should all close your eyes?" It is best imagined how quickly I obeyed that order. My eyelashes might have as well lit a fire with that speed.

Thwack! The first feel of the hard wood against my soft buttocks convinced me that I had just lost use of my legs. A sharply delivered second blow to my back immediately killed any sensory nerves I had so I did not know when I had received my own share of the six strokes. My hands seemed to suddenly loose the urge to live as my grip on the pole loosened and I sunk to the ground. Never in my twelve years of existence had I felt so much pain. I must have drifted into a swift doze because by the time Peter shook my shoulders for me to go to classroom; Joseph had flogged all twelve of us and gone to his room.

I literally dragged myself to my classroom but tried as much as possible to maintain a straight face for the prying eyes that wondered why I was just entering the class at the end of the second period.

Bode's sympathetic face greeted me when I got to my seat.

"Sorry" He said, as I praised God that I sat with Bode and not with Victor.

Mrs. Olagunju was our social studies teacher. She was a straight –faced, matter-of-fact woman. She was the perfect blend of African and European culture. She was also the reason many of my mates stood in front of the mirror everyday twisting nose, mouth and all, in a desperate attempt to speak English the way she did.

She walked into the class at 9.00 a.m. on the dot at barely the same time the blaring sirens from the administrative block indicated that it was the beginning of a new period.

"Saheed, out!" She said immediately she entered, ignoring our greetings. Saheed, in his usual manner bounced out of the class damning the consequences. He was Mrs. Olagunju's number one enemy. Other students who were doing things that they knew would offend the woman immediately reconsidered their positions.

"Ranti, don't bother yourself. Pick up the chewing gum from the floor" Mrs. Olagunju pointed at the exact spot where the girl threw the gum.

"Now get up"

A pale-faced girl stood up at the centre of the class. Had it not been Mrs. Olagunju who was talking, I might have suggested that the girl had been falsely accused because of the look on her face.

"Now get out!"

Ranti walked briskly out of the class face down. It was the first time an adult had spoken harshly to her since the day she was born.

"As for you two, Biodun and Dolapo, I'll assume I did not see you laughing" The two boys mentioned immediately acquired countenances soberer than that of Tibetan monks.

She walked smartly to the middle of the classroom to demand chalk from the appointed chalk boy, "Okay. Pens out. Topic is Rural-Urban Migration. Do not forget. All your topics must be in capital letters and neatly underlined. Otherwise..." She only waved her fingers then sighed. I quickly got my note and Bic biro out and tried to scribble something down but what I wrote certainly did not seem to be in English language. It looked more like something written in Arabic. My biro moved unsteadily between my thumb and forefinger. My right hand was particularly very heavy from all what transpired between Chike and me the night before.

He asked me to lie astride a gutter behind the S.S.3 dormitory after literally dragging me from my hostel around 11.45 p.m. Prior to his coming to call me, he had collected about 15 of the toughest leather belts ever made and placed it on a near-by suck-away. By the side of the belts were a rechargeable lantern and two packs of Five-Alive juice. In his left hand was his Government notebook. I guess you get the picture.

While fumes of urine and every sort of rubbish present in Federal Government College, Lagos tortured my nose, Chike read his note and drank juice! He sat cross-legged and sipped from the pack as if oblivious of the fact that both of my hands clutched to the concrete on both sides of the gutter as if for dear life. The last thing I wanted in my second year in this school was a bath in about the filthiest gutter in the whole of West Africa.

I therefore believe you would see reason with me when at the lapse of fifty-two minutes, I pushed myself up and started walking away, grumbling that I couldn't serve that punishment again. A thousand poets cannot adequately explain what happened next. Common! Who can vividly describe the agility Chike displayed when he stood up from the suckaway and caught up with me in a split second? The strength he displayed when he carried me by my collar with a single lift of his left hand or the athletic powers he showed when he tossed me about seven feet from the sandy area behind the hostel to the hard, concrete, suck-away. Now tell me what Hollywood hunk can replicate the human attributes of Chike when he picked up about four belts at the same time and lashed me on spots I never knew even existed? Up till now, I really do not know how I got to my bed because the last thing I could recall was Chike's final slap carefully delivered to my supple cheeks

Come to think of it. I thought I saw...

"Wake up!" Little did I know that Mrs. Olagunju had just knocked my head twice in a bid to wake me up.

"What is your problem?" She asked when my two gummy eyes tried to free themselves.

"He is not feeling well" Bode had immediately answered on my behalf. It was at times like this I mostly valued my friendship with Bode. Even if he said there was a blue sun in the sky, every teacher and even our stern principal would not hesitate before they believed what he said was true. As far as they were concerned, Bode was the only truthful student in the school. It is of no surprise therefore that Mrs. Olagunju actually told me sorry before continuing with the lesson.

****

"Come, whoever owns this singlet should better remove it before I move it" Tunji said

"Ahh!! Victor screamed as if he had found the missing part of his brain. Whoever owns it should better remove it before Tunji moves it because when Tunji moves something...hmm...the thing has gone to the land of no return oh!"

Tunji looked at Victor then smiled. The whole room spoke along with him as he started his usual doctrine.

"Stealing is a game, but when caught, it is a crime."

"Whisky!!!" Someone screamed from behind. Tunji's head almost burst open. As far as he was concerned, the best compliment you could give him was to call him 'whisky'. There was nothing like appreciating his speed, his ability to 'whisk' things away and not be seen. There was no greater challenge than to ask him to walk briskly through a room and ensure that two pairs of uniforms got missing. It was here I came in.

"Tunji" I called him from my bed, from where I had been observing what it was like to be without worries in the eyes of everyone else.

"What's up?" He asked.

"I hung Chike's baffs above where you were sitting just now yesterday afternoon. I went to play a game but..."

"I didn't take it" He interrupted me. "Serious" He added when he saw the look on my face.

"Please now. Do you want Chike to kill me? The guy beat the hell out of me yesterday and I guess he is returning today."

"I'm serious" Tunji said again. I quite believed him. He only stole for fun and recognition. In most cases, he always returned the things he stole on the condition that the owner acknowledged his prowess. I used to call him Thomas Crown before, but dropped the name when I noticed that he really didn't understand the joke.

"I suspect Isioma"

I looked at Tunji.

"It's like you think I am joking about the clothes."

He hissed and started to walk away but I held him back when I realized that he seemed to mean what he said.

"Wait now" I pleaded. "The thing is that Isioma and I were playing Ijanikin Soccer when it was stolen"

"Bone that side. What if he sent someone to take it saying it was his? Or what if he even did it himself? Listen, you guys don't know that boy, he is a bloody criminal."

I was obliged to believe him for the mere fact that he acknowledged that there was someone in this dormitory who was better than him when it came to stealing.

"Did the guy leave at all when you guys were playing?"

I thought for a moment then said no. "But then, why do you suspect him so strongly? After all, virtually everybody in this dormitory is a potential thief. Why him?"

"I saw him talking to Chike about an hour after the baffs were stolen"

Tunji stood up. "Think about it" He said, and then walked away.

That was exactly what I did. I thought about it. The first problem worth thinking about was how Tunji knew the exact time the clothes were stolen. Naturally, he had just replaced Isioma in the number spot.

I caught sight of Isioma from the corner of my eye as he walked grudgingly into the room. Isioma always dragged his feet when he walked. His hair was always unkempt and bushy, his shirt tucked out and his eyes permanently wide open. Isioma was the kind of guy who set his eyes on something, then went out to get it at all cost, ignoring all forms of intuition and conscience. His elder brother, who also finished from a Federal Government College in another state, told him there were two types of people in a boarding house. Those that survived, and those that didn't. He had further explained that by the word survive, he meant the thin line between those that beat others, and those that were beaten; Those who cried all the time, and those who had something new to smile about; Those who stole, and those from whom things were stolen. Isioma had therefore travelled the seventy-five kilometres from his house to F.G.C.L. Ijanikin to survive, and nothing more.

"How far? Shey you don see the baffs?"

I looked wearily at Isioma. I wondered if he was smart enough to see the mistrust in my eyes.

"No" I tried to make my voice steady. If this was a game, I certainly did not want to be the loser.

"What were you asking Rakim and Jide?" He was obviously startled by my question.

"When?" Isioma asked. "A few minutes ago. I saw you asking them about something when you entered."

"O! I dey ask them about...ass...assignment"

"Uhn? I did not need Bode's brains to know that bothering about an assignment was the last thing Isioma would use his time for.

"You ke? Assignment?" I asked again laughing.

Isioma laughed rather forcibly. "I just dey joke. Oh! So wetin you mean? Say I no fit ask person for assignment, say na only play I know?" Apparently, Isioma had a good sense of what he was all about.

"Don't play me. What were you asking them for?" I asked, suddenly serious.

"Wetin dey freak you sef?" Isioma was clearly getting impatient with me.

"Okay, make I yarn you. I dey find something."

"What?"

Isioma hissed irritably. "See, if na say you dey suspect me for that stuff. Stop am. How many times I go yarn you say no be me..."

"That's a lie. I've never asked you..." I tried cutting in but Isioma continued, "No be both of us dey play game together. In short, make I talk true. The person wey I suspect na Whisky. I see am and Chike dey talk before I come jam you make we play."

19th November

Last night, I unbuttoned my shirt, loosened my belt then set them all on the bed. My mind was totally occupied on the mind maze I found myself in along with the three most terrible people I had ever had to deal with since I set my tiny feet across the gates of this school. The three guys were Isioma, Whisky and of course, the devil-incarnate himself; the first son of the inferno underground; Reverendevil. For the sake of obscenities, I think we should stick with Chike. Yes, Chike.

That however was not the name on the collar of the blue-checked shirt I had just picked from my bed, that one read Tayo, written in italics. I recalled the trouble my mom took to carefully inscribe the name with a red thread to reduce the chances of it getting stolen. This was the reason why I carefully hung it on the same hanger where my brown Khaki trousers had made itself at home. I placed the pair at the edge of the burglary proof nearest my bed and made sure my wooden locker totally covered it. The next thing I did was to reverently dust the sand off my green bathroom slippers, and then place it under my mattress at the spot where my head also lay. Before anybody would be able to steal my slippers, he would have to be blessed with the talents of the dreaded *Anini* of before and the swiftness of Whisky.

By now all I had on was my most expensive underwear ever- a BYC singlet and my boxers. I decided I needed a little rest before pulling out my metallic box to retrieve my pyjamas. That idea however turned out to be a bad one. It was a mistake I constantly made because as usual, I always slept off in less than twenty minutes. I mean, totally dozed off.

I'm a guy of little words so ***what exactly is my point?!!!!***

My point? All right, I'll tell you. It was what I had on when I slept, hence what I had on when I awoke- A white singlet and boxers alone.

"Come, where this guy, em... Tayo?"

Before I left home for each term, I was constantly bathed in prayers from family, friends, and church to make sure I came back home with every single part of my body intact. No wonder immediately that sentence was spoken, some unseen forces (I would like to believe they were angels) woke me up and literally sang one of my most dreaded lullabies in my ears. It goes thus: *there is fire on the mountain, run...**run**...**Run!***

It was about 5.15 in the morning so no one was awake as the poles were usually banged at 5.45 am. Come to think of it, the gates to the dormitory could not have been opened yet! One more look at Chike's long, strong, muscular legs and I knew just how he entered.

"Run down, you bastard!" He barked, as he set foot in my room.

As if by magic, pangs of pain from my ordeal with this demon two nights ago resurfaced on my back, so I simply obeyed Chike- I ran, but it was neither up nor down, I ran far away from him, far...far...away. I guess it was either because he was surprised that I could still dare to run after the lesson he taught me the other night that he hesitated before pursuing me. Or maybe the unforeseen forces I mentioned earlier on were really at work, because my legs had just started moving faster than the tires of the latest Ferrari. I dashed into room four through the door that connected my room with theirs, and then literally glided to the dormitory corridors after kicking open their door.

Hey! See this boy, u dey craze?" Chike screamed in the only language he knew how to speak behind me. But of course, I would be the worst fool on Earth if I dared stop to give a reply to his question. Not only that, I would become a bearer of the dreaded title 'late'. The bathroom was made up of several small compartments with no roof atop. That was why I sprinted straight into it without even considering it might end up being a dead end for me. As I jumped to the top of one of the compartments, climbed unto the wall of the dormitory then got outside the dormitory, I made a mental note to write a memo to our principal on the security of students in the J.S.S 2 dormitory when all this was over, if all these ever got over. This was because under three seconds, I had scaled out of the dormitory! This was an art I always believed could be practiced by only the leggy S.S 3 boys. But then, maybe it was just the 'forces' again.

Meanwhile, Chike was giving me a hot chase. I could hear him breathing heavily a few metres behind me. I meandered between the extension and J.S.S 3 hostels. Reverendevil was closing the gap very steadily. His long legs were stretching out one after the other like that of Michael Johnson as he cursed his way closer to me. The air outside was misty and chilling but this was not the time to think about cardigans. In no time at all, I was on the main road that led to the school field. I could see some people running from the class area towards their dormitory. A number of junior students usually went to the blocks of taps situated near the classes to bathe. This was because fetching water from there and carrying it to the dormitory to bathe would simply be a humanitarian effort as seniors were sure to hijack you along the way. If you were really lucky, you would leave with your bucket. Then you would either have to beg your way into getting a bath that morning or employ the legendary techniques of 'Rub and shine', a technique in which I already had a master's degree. As I looked on these boys, a forlorn expression settled on my face. I wished the reason I was also running was to avoid girls seeing me in my underwear. I would give a finger for that. It was at this point that I remembered why I was outside by 5. 20a.m-Chike! Where was he? He was no longer behind me. Had he given up on me? Did he think I wasn't worth the chase or sweat? Or had he gone to recruit his other mates who were as hardened as he was to assist him with his breakfast...my heart?

Suddenly! A creature jumped in my direction. It was big, very big. It had long legs that seemed to dispute Newton's laws of gravitation. It appeared they were gliding through the air as they flew in my direction. The outstretched arms that were obviously attracted to my necks were hairy, and muscular. They looked somewhat familiar. Then I immediately remembered where I had seen them before. We met once, and I remembered it was not exactly a pleasant experience. They had slapped me several times two nights ago and swung a leathery substance till my back stung like bees had a feast there. They were Chike's. I was not an acrobat. I had never practiced martial arts, and though on several occasions after watching a Jet-li film, I wished we were cousins, or at least family friends, I knew the possibilities were slimmer than Fela. So, you see, I really don't know how it became that out of the blue; I was suddenly standing a few feet from a soakaway that nanoseconds earlier I had my back to. Was something strange happening to me? Had I acquired magical powers that had been lost in my lineage generations earlier? Because I would sure like to practice some tricks on this guy chasing me. Then I remembered that was only a popular Hollywood concept. A world neither Chike nor I resided. Back to the real world, I noticed that I was standing in front of the mosque. The mosque was like the notorious Olumo Rock of Abeokuta that served as a refuge to people during the war between the Moranike tribe and another my mind was not in the mood to recollect. What a coincidence, because I was in a war myself. A war in which victory meant I survived- at least today- without getting shredded to pieces. All Moslems among the students frowned at improper dressing or attitude by anybody once he was standing on the same soil that housed the holy place. Surprisingly, Chike stopped. I had no idea he believed in the existence of a God, or rules of any sort. Well, what do you know, the devil, probably more than anyone on Earth knows God. He turned back and started walking back to his hostel. Maybe today was not the day I was to die. I started singing hymns in my mind. I would definitely give a testimony next Sunday, I thought. But I was dead wrong, or right as the case may be- as far as Chike was concerned, which student would reprimand him for committing murder in the mosque? Some teachers even avoided situations where Chike would do something they should normally correct him for. He was simply to be avoided. It was students like this who got recruited to be hired assassins immediately they were through schooling. No sooner had Chike turned away from me before he made a screeching U-turn. I'm not sure if I was imagining it or not but

Chike seemed to be moving faster, chasing harder. I guess in that split second when he stopped, his resolve to commit murder as the first thing this morning quadrupled. That left me with two bad options and one terrible one: I either run into the thick forest that bordered most of our school, with all the mystery surrounding it; run towards the classes giving Chike's long legs ample opportunity to catch up with me; or simply stop running, drop to my knees and tell Reverendevil that I had sinned against humanity, heaven and him, and simply did not deserve to live. I could almost feel Chike's bodily heat as he would descend on me if I decided to go with plan C. Plan A was it.

I dashed towards the forest like it was my spirit trying to leave my body. I ran into the darkness it offered as comfort like it was my saviour calling me into the light. I ran into the evil forest that had at its evil middle the famous cashew bush like it was where I had always wanted to be. A thought struck me as my legs spun me into the thickness of a forest I had once dreaded like AIDS- If this forest was evil, and Chike was devil's representative in this school, did it not follow that he would know the Cashew bush like the back of his palms? I was going to put that idea to the test as I made a sudden turn that led me deeper away from light and into the forest. It did not matter that I was breathing like a dragon, the only thing I could hear right now was Chike's laborious steps as he definitely tried to crack the code that made me invincible and difficult to catch today. I imagined the time was now around 7.30 a.m. because I could hear the clanking of plates in the dining hall. This thought reminded my stomach that it had not been fed that morning and it immediately began to ache for food. However, on hearing quick long footsteps coming towards me through the darkness of the forest, the clamours for breakfast were immediately forgotten.

This was my second time in this forest. The first time was when I was in my first year in this school. It was on a Saturday. I did not get to eat any breakfast that morning because I was not among the first four people on the table, so I had to come with a friend to get food 'garden-of-Eden style'. In the dining hall, we were arranged according to our classes. Hence every male J.S.S. 1 student ate in the same wing of the dining hall. We were further divided into groups of ten to constitute a table. On tables filled with *diners* (These were students who were very efficient in getting optimal food in the dining hall), there were codes of honour. On my table for instance, the first person to get to the table took half of the food; if the second person was extremely nice, he divided the remaining half into two portions that he and the third person shared. Consequently, you see why I tried to be friendly with as many people as possible, or how on Earth was I to survive the whole term on Garri a.k.a garium sulphate?

Right now, I could no longer hear Chike behind me but that did not necessarily mean the murderer was not at large. A fresh, juicy Cashew stared at me from a nearby tree like the apple stared at Eve in the beginning. I immediately understood the way Eve must have felt then when without premeditation, I immediately started climbing the tree branch by branch. The time was probably 9 a.m. already and I had not gotten a morsel of anything to eat at all! I was so famished that even seeing Chike waiting at the bottom of the tree for me to descend into pain did not stop my teeth from biting into the juicy, red cashew. He motioned gently that I should come down. I took in the situation and decided that the only way I could escape him this time would involve one of my legs getting broken if I tried to jump and run. But what use will that be any way, because he was sure to catch me all the same and inflict even a double portion of pain. I remembered watching the film, 'The Negotiator'. I tried to recollect what the actor did when faced with a terrorist. I remember he usually talked slowly and gently before pulling a fast one on the boss. I however did not have a gun, and either way, how gently could I talk to soothe Chike. He was presently smiling at me from the corner of his lips as his right hand curved into the biggest fist I had ever seen. Suddenly I realised I was hearing something other than the thumping of my heart.

"Na dem be that! Catch them! Make dem no escape! Computer cover that side!"

Before I could put two and two together to give four I realised that we had just been besieged by 'Gados'. A hallelujah chorus surfaced on my lips, but fear will not let any music be sung. The 'Gados were the security men of the school. There were about five of them; Parieé, Computer, S. killer (I always wondered if the 'S' stood for student), and two others whose names I could not remember. They were employed after a robbery attempt was allegedly made by some ex-students. Thus, I guess they were employed with the objectives of catching, maiming and diffusing those among us who had decided to become dynamites. I wondered if their rounding up on Chike and I right now meant I had joint the league of the notorious students to be weary of. No. I did not think so. This was just like the movies where the undercover cop was supposedly arrested along with the culprit, so the drug dealer would not know who snitched on him. The undercover cop was usually released immediately...

"Na the Tayo be that. Na fast runner o! Computer hold am well-well!" Parieé was seriously barking orders at the gado that was now holding me by the singlet like I was the man he heard was caught red-handed in bed with his wife. Inasmuch as I feared Parieé, I had little regard for Computer especially considering the source of his name. It was said that the first time he saw a computer, he fainted-I wondered if there was any truth to that story. Could someone be so disconnected from the real world?

On the other hand, I feared Parieé like fire. Legend had it that he was trained as a dangerous hunter in the forests of Ijebu Igbo. It was said and believed that his master was a dangerous *juju* man who bewitched Parieé to tear the mouth of his prey immediately his name was called.

Parieé! Another gado called from inside the guardroom that we were approaching. My mouth was left ajar as I turned to regard Chike's mouth...

Don't worry, I too would have loved to see it happen, but nothing happened to Chike's mouth. Parieé had his eyes locked on me instead of tearing mouths. I wonder who it was that spread all those ridiculous rumours. Chike on the other hand was staring at me from the depths of his eyes with hatred that had definitely multiplied by the hundreds. We were brusquely thrown into two separate rooms in the guardroom. The guardroom of this college was the equivalent of the cells in the real world where students like Chike and I were kept before being 'tried' in the disciplinary unit headed by the rightly dreaded Mr. Akpan. Mr. Akpan was six foot three with tribal marks that stopped his face from smiling and a constant smell of stale sweat. He always looked agitated and sweaty like he had just finished a workout. I guess he needed all the energy he could muster considering the vital role he played among the teachers- He was the flogging machine of the school! He had gifted hands that knew the exact curves on the buttocks of students that elicited the most pain when hit. He knew how to swing his *'Pankéré'* (The stick used to beat students) with the kind of mathematical precision that made students confess to crimes they knew nothing about. Would I have the rare privilege of getting on a first name basis with his right hand in a few moments? This was because if found guilty at the disciplinary unit, the next step was a quick dose of cane from 'The marked man', as we fondly called him.

Usually, if it was on a Monday or Thursday, when we had the general assembly and block assembly respectively, the 'suspects' were usually paraded in front of the students. For goodness sake! What will Bisi think of me if I was brought out and flogged on the assembly ground like a common criminal? Will my chances with her be jeopardized for the flimsy excuse that I ran because a Leopard was pursuing me? Who would believe that? All these questions pointed at only one common fact: That I either intensified my prayers that I was released from this jail, or that I... Even the sheer thought was scary...run away!

When I came to after a few hours of a sudden wave of sleep that overwhelmed me, I took in my surroundings. I was in a small, dark room with no windows (No wonder I was sweating so profusely), and a heavy wooden door that manned what was obviously the only inlet into the room. I remembered being chased by Chike, getting manhandled by Computer, then finally getting thrown into this shit hole like an unwanted luggage. I still could not figure out why they knew my name. I wondered what the time was. Today being Friday meant that school was going to end earlier. It also meant an apparently missed meal of rice, stew and meat which I spent the entire week looking forward to because it was one of those rear occasions where we were fed meat (That's if I made it as one of the 1st three people on the table, of course). Pangs of hunger suddenly tore at me from my insides, making me realise that I had only eaten two helpings of Cashew today. It was somewhat hard to believe it was my stomach making the growling sounds I could hear in short, sustained quips. I listened carefully. What I realised almost made me puke out of sheer disgust! It was Chike! It appeared he was in the room next to mine and was most likely threatening me.

"I go chop you like groundnut" He muttered under his breath, then added for illustration, "Chok, chok, chok"

"You think say na you go ruin me for this school? You never even jam. That evil spirit wey dey inside you wey dey make...in short I no fi shout. Sha run when you get chance, if not..."

I felt like laughing when he said those words, because I was also planning how to ruin him. All I needed was a shot with those disciplinary guys, so I could give a mind blowing account of how this whole thing started. As an introduction, I would mention in my most impeccable Queen's English how this boy has constantly terrorized students and staff alike (I hoped I would have Mr. Ude's corroboration on this one, because the man was still scared stiff of the boy.) My scheming was put to an end when I heard stamping of feet that appeared to lead their owners to my door.

Parieé and Computer entered my small apartment with the solemn look of undertakers. Parieé was the taller of the two with broad muscled arms that looked like they could lift a cow. Computer on the other hand was slim built with a lean face and small, intense eyes. He spoke first in surprisingly good English.

"Tayo. The game is over. We've been watching you for a while and know you know. Where is the body?"

I wondered if I had an innate ability to understand the language he was speaking because they sounded logical yet did not make sense. What did they mean by body? Wait! I think I have gotten it! This was a trance. I was seeing through the eyes of Chike and they were asking him where he hid my body after killing me.

I snapped out of the daydream when Parieé stooped beside me, so I could smell the weed in his breath and asked me like a no-nonsense detective where the body was. My mind began to spin as different thoughts crossed my mind. Was there any other Tayo in my class who these dudes seemed to have me mistaken for? They sounded as if they had rounded me up in the dormitory to ask me 'routine' questions. Anyway, what did they mean by body? I could not recollect any student who was looking for his body as silly as that sounded. Then the thought struck me like lightening witches had prepared to hit me, maybe there was a missing body after all. That girl...

A whistle was forcefully blown thrice somewhere in the distance. It must have indicated that there was an emergency situation somewhere that concerned them because they immediately turned from me and sprinted towards the sound. I was able to pick out the time from Computer's rubber strapped wrist watch. It indicated that it was around 4.30 p.m. This meant that students were now having their afternoon prep. Our guidance and counselling teachers usually theorized that we were to use our afternoon prep to review what we had done during the day and to battle any assignments the day had left us with. Well, that was the ideal school they usually fantasized about. But even life itself is never ideal. Hence, rather than review schoolwork, in the absence of supervisors, students spent the time reviewing events of the day resulting in enough chit chat to make market women green with envy. I guessed this defined peculiarity of the afternoon prep classes had something to do with the sudden flight from my cell.

Barely two minutes after the gados fled from me, Victor appeared in front of my door. Like he must have felt several times, I wanted to ask a million questions. And like I must have usually acted in return, He immediately started to talk condescendingly.

"I can't say much now because of time. It is Isioma and whisky that you have to thank for the gados leaving. They were fighting over your supposed assumption that one of them stole Chike's baffs from you. Meanwhile, I brought you your house wear, some biscuits and water."

"When did they start fighting?" I asked noncommittally. Meanwhile, I tried to break the record of how many sticks of biscuit could be shoved into the mouth as once.

"Just now" Victor replied immediately, certainly impressed that he actually did have some answers after all.

"Then that will mean you are just coming from the hostel with all these stuffs you brought for me." I was eager to continue the natter, so I won't look as overcome with the food as I felt it definitely appeared. After a minute, I realised Victor had not answered my question, which was strange. I was about to word it again when it became obvious he was fumbling for the answer like he was about to tell a lie, something I once swore he had never done before in his life.

"I..." The words failed him. "Eh!" He exclaimed forcefully. "They are coming back. He briskly walked out of the guardroom like he had to use the restroom.

True to his words, the gados were on their way; just that it appeared Victor had started seeing five minutes into the future. That made me seriously wonder what had got him so worked up that he committed his very own unforgivable sin- never to lie. I was still trying to figure this out when Parieé and Computer got back with two squabbling teenagers I presumed to be Isioma and Whisky. It appeared they had started fighting again because I could hear the gados cursing and slapping as they tried to separate them in the adjacent room.

"Sharaap! Shey I talk say make you talk?" That was Parieé yapping. "By the way," He continued, "Wetin cause all this wahala sef?"

"Na Whisky" Naturally, that was the fast talking Isioma.

"Chike talk say make we do one simple thing for am with one guy na him this guy say make we go tell…"

"Sharaap!" Parieé barked again "Who you think say you dey fool with all this your guy-guy talk. You better behave or…" He raised his backhand towards Isioma in an attempt to give a slap he obviously already planned not to give.

"About Three days ago…" Whisky had started a story I guess he had been trying to tell the guy Isioma spoke about. What I did not know was that as the story unfolded, my heartbeat would climb like a plane taking off with each word he spoke…

Judging by the darkness outside, I guessed the time was around 8p.m. I had just walloped the only meal an inmate in this prison of sorts was allowed to have. I was fed an ant sized lump of *eba* and enough *egusi* soup to merely smear the plate. Don't bother about how ungrateful I sound, I devoured the whole concoct greedily all the same. With all the philosophy I could muster, I decided to name today 'the day of mysteries almost solved'. What with the accusation that I somehow knew the whereabouts of that weird girl (Chike was not asked the same questions or any at all. I guess they just wanted him where he could be prevented from wreaking havoc); the revelation that the clothes that were missing had gotten safely tucked away by the trio of Chike, Whisky and Isioma for the sake of a game I still found hard to comprehend; and the sudden, inexplicable change in Victor. Today had certainly turned out to be the weirdest I've lived in a long while. Something struck me. The last four days of my life have been beguiled by one problem or another like I was under some curse. I cast my mind back to the midterm holidays that just ended. Did I do anything off beam? Curse the name of a god? Insult my mother under my breadth?

These thoughts flooded my mind as I tried to solve the riddle of these mishaps in my life. As usual though, another sudden occurrence stopped my brainstorming. Before I go into that, I must apologise for my ill manners. I did not introduce you to the guardroom I've been forced to make my home. It was a small three-bedroom apartment at the gate to the college. I have always argued that situating it at the entrance of the school- the visitor's first contact with this institution, was insane. It was like washing dirty linen in public. The first room led to the other two rooms. This was where the guards stayed. From here, a narrow corridor gave rise to two adjacent rooms that housed Chike and I.

This means that when I heard a whistle, then the scuttling of feet as one of the guards rushed in the direction of the sound, I was surprised to hear three more things in quick succession. First, a door I desperately feared was Chike's opened and closed very quickly. Next, I heard Parieé open his mouth to order an inmate to his cell but instead the words that ended up coming out were a soft, surprised moan of "Ahh!" The third thing there was to hear was my door getting opened to reveal the dark, piercing eyes of the person that freed me so he could kill me.

Wait a minute! I almost said. Wasn't I supposed to get an apology for the whole trouble this guy had put me through for nothing at all?

As if he could read my thoughts, He said something that almost split my mind into pieces. "The baffs dey with me. So what?"

"Run!"

If I wanted to think this through I would not have moved an inch because as Chike said those words, he excused me so I could pass. There was however an evil smile spread across his chapped lips. I ran. Like a mad woman.

When my legs started moving, I did not even think about where I was going. However, several things raced across my mind that promised to give me insight. One was what was Reverendevil up to? Secondly, I knew I could not go to my hostel because I had just escaped from the guardroom. Was that not like the most heinous crime a student could commit? But another argument came into mind. These gados appeared to be playing by their own rules. It did not make sense that they did not take us to the disciplinary committee. Or did those disciplinary guys order the harsh treatment we just received? It did not seem likely. A Yoruba proverb said that no matter what a child did, no Father would beat him to death. Then two thoughts clashed across my mind before bouncing back with such force, it almost split my brains. It did not make sense that a student would be accused of the mysterious disappearance of the girl I guessed they were questioning me about. That meant that these gados were up to something. Something dangerous.

I suddenly realised that as I ran, a familiar stiletto was also running like a cheetah towards me.

"Na you sabi run abi?" The voice called out breathlessly. "Oya make we see. Na u be hider, na me be seeker, and for my village, the seekers dey kill wetin dem dey find wen they catch am. Make I no catch you"

Chike's threat brought out energy in me that I never knew existed as I ran once more into the place I was going to spend the next three days of my life. In my usual carefree manner, a silly thought crept into my mind. It was the realisation that I was obviously a good runner because I could hear Chike panting heavily into cries of the night. It made me feel good that at this rate, Mike Tyson was more likely to beat Holyfield than Chike catch me. What I did not bargain for was the stone that he had just sent flying towards my head. When it hit its target, I heard a sudden pop in my head, like tiny dynamites exploded inside my skull. Next was darkness. And a World that would not stop spinning.

20th November

I changed gear as I negotiated one last bend on the way to my house. The journey home had been tasking; one road block after another. One policeman did not let me move till I settled him. Shortly after that, some armed robbers tried to snatch the car from me but I was not fazed. When they pumped three bullets into my skull and I still did not move, they knew I would not give up the car at any cost. As if that was not enough for one journey, I had also driven headlong into a gigantic trailer, but the super glue in my pocket quickly repaired the damage to the car. I could not risk my dad finding out I had taken his last child, Mazda 306, to school, I needed some 'Abracadabra', fast! What I did was simple, when I got to the gate; I turned off the ignition, removed the key, then safely tucked the car into my pockets. With any luck, neither of my parents would have realised their most expensive toy was missing. That was the way it turned out.

I got to the gate, careful not to wake the principal who usually stood in for our gateman during the holidays. I then gently brought out the blue car from my back pocket; making sure the horn was not pressed in the process. Once I parked it properly, I started to heave a sigh of relief when I felt my dad's hard palm on my cheeks, and he was not saying hi. He was delivering quick, heavy slaps in succession so I could realise the gravity of what I had done- "Who asked me to give birth to my junior brother?" He seemed to be asking. "Did he not say my fast clothes were going to die?"

My JAMB questions appeared to get even harder from one paper to another. I was on my third. The first question looked familiar, but I could not remember which school said it: "What will save me from this evil forest?" It asked...

When my eyes opened, one heavy eyelid after another, I saw Chike brandishing his belt before my eyes. And then my dreams started to make sense.

"So u don finally wake up abi? I think say you don pa already. Take position..."

I stood up, adjusted my trouser, then my shir... Five fingers spread across my face like the oceans cover the Earth.

"Shey na me you dey use shine. Shey I tell you say you dey go fashion runway way u dey dress your...In short take position now!" He billowed.

Without further ado I immediately bent over double with my buttocks towards his face. I just wished my sphincters would let go so I could at least give him some shit too. 'Position' is a stance someone could be asked to take when beaten in this school. Its knowledge was passed from one generation of seniors to another. The subject was usually asked to bend at his waist till his fingers touched his toes. The 'slave master' would then flog with a stick, ensuring that his cane hit just the outermost curve of the buttocks of his prey. It was designed to cause optimal pain-After twelve strokes from Chike, believe me when I say those who designed it achieved their objective.

I felt like I had been run over by a trailer, and then jumped upon by an elephant. I felt awful.

"You know wetin dey funny me pass?" Chike asked, but he obviously was not looking for an answer because he added immediately, "you no do me anything, yet I just hate you" He spat. He spun around suddenly and delivered another high five on my face. His long, slender fingers made me see stars.

A familiar feeling came over me, Darkness, darkness, then total black out.

"You think say you wise abi?" Mrs Olagunju asked with hatred. I was scared. What was happening? When did she begin to speak pidgin English? But that did not surprise me as much as what happened next. Bode appeared from nowhere and suddenly started dealing blows to every inch of my body. He was also speaking pidgin English. "If you like faint ten times, I go still torture you. You wan coba me abi? Make dat...wetin im be self, come spoil my life? I go torture you. If you like die. Anyway, dem don talk say the thing no go kill you" Each word ended with a blow or slap to some hidden part of my body. It was like he was trying to calculate the total surface area of my body. Wait! I almost said. Wasn't there a scientific and pain free way of calculating those kinds of things. Immediately I said this, Mr. Tubosun, the integrated science teacher slapped me again. He asked me several questions in a row. Each question ended with either a blow or another slap. Then I drifted again. This time I saw Dare, my childhood friend. He was calling me outside to play. For years, we played together in the sands, climbed trees and cried over our report cards. He looked me in the eye, said something quick and harsh, and... You guessed right...He gave me a slap on both sides of my cheeks in quick succession...

I opened my eyes uneasily. It was like I was being drawn over and over again into a vortex of pain. Why was this happening to me? I asked for the umpteenth time. The forest seemed darker now than what I could remember. It was like crickets had taken residence in my ears, the sound they made undulated in intensity. Finally, my ears settled on my captive. He was grinning. My eyes followed his hands as they led to a small piece of bread and a sachet of pure water beside my foot. Did his friends from the underground bring these? Were they trying to drug me? Well these were the questions my head was asking. Is it not said that the head directs the activities of the body. Maybe there was a dysfunction in my case, because while my head was saying: 'Don't eat!' 'Don't eat!' my stomach, on the other hand, appearing to swim in poison was saying: 'Eat! Anything at all!' My hands did not even wait for the rest of my body before they dived to the bread and tried to shove all of it at once into my mouth. I was simultaneously eating and drinking water at once like I had just been freed from 'Kirikiri' where I hear people are sentenced to starve to death from all over the world. Chike was observing the situation with relish. What he did next was...I'll leave you to be the judge...

I had hardly gone halfway through my meal when he suddenly rushed at me, shouting like we were red Indians at war. He started pummelling me with punches. It appeared he was particularly trying to get the food out of my stomach. He threw little fists of fire into my stomach, one violent fist after another. When I opened my mouth to throw up what he would not let me get in, he clutched my neck like a chicken's. When he was satisfied I was not going to throw up again. He started again, ramming even more punches into my stomach. He stopped suddenly. Not just him. Everything stopped. A deep growl sounded somewhere from the rear. We both turned around to see a tiger staring menacingly deep into our eyes or was it our flesh.

Again, that rhyme came to mind: 'Fire on the mountain. Run, Run, Run!

I ran.

Like the devil was trying to make friends with me. Chike, on the other hand too took off in the opposite direction. I guess that was what confused the tiger, who would it pursue, it seemed to ask itself. That question unfortunately did not take long to answer, because in a few seconds, I heard animal like panting a few paces behind me. The tiger had chosen me for the sacrifice.

I dashed for what I hoped were the outlines of the forest, but everything seemed to have changed. The forest, myself, the world. What the hell was happening? How did a tiger even end up in the school premises? I ran harder, dashing from one tree to another. The tiger sounded even closer behind me.

"Grrr" It was saying. I wondered if 'Grr' meant 'Come, let me have a word with you', or 'don't worry, I'm not gonna bite you', or maybe it meant: 'Hey! Give me a break, I'm just trying to have diner here'. Either way, I ran. I was running out of breath and my head was getting light. My sight was failing me, everything was taking up a grey hue. I did not see the thick branch of a huge tree hanging out like a chain, so I ran headlong into it; it felt metallic against my soft forehead. Everything in the world got greyer, then black, then silence, then darkness.

21st November

When I awoke, my head was banging terribly like someone was drilling a hole at the sides of my head. That made me smile. When I finally wake up, I thought, I'd share my story with my roommates. I would title it 'the most ridiculous dream of the century'. Who knows, it might be made into a film, and I might win an Oscar for best scriptwriter, and be a superstar, and all that.

My eyes gradually began to see things singly as I adjusted to the world after a nightmare-filled night. When they did finally open I wished I had my super glue with me-so I could keep them closed...forever

Grinning at me like a shy boy with a chick was Victor.

"Awake?" He asked. What an irony, I thought. I was in some remote part of the forest beside the very tree whose branch had brought me down. I suddenly shivered when I remembered Chike. Victor seemed to know what I was thinking. "Don't worry about him" He said like an old nanny. "We have a long day ahead." He added.

Something, sorry, everything about Victor had changed. What the hell has happened to Victor? I asked in my head, almost hysterical. He was wearing his house wear. The hem of his brown khaki had been folded several times and his feet and fingers were soiled, like he had playing in the sand.

"First, food" Victor said, oblivious to the quizzical look in my eyes. He grabbed my right hand and started leading me to parts of the forest I had never seen before, despite my several trips to this same forest in search for ripe cashew. I wanted to protest about being led like a dog, but then I remembered we were searching for food, and pardon me, but this guy, whoever he really was, seemed to know his way around. Food, remember? I reminded the part of me that was screaming: Code red!

We finally got to where he was leading me because he stopped and pointed. I almost screamed with fright when I stared into what was supposed to be Victor's eyes. They were opened wide, as in fright, and were the dirtiest shade of brown I had ever seen before. Equally stunning was what he was pointing at- A corner of the forest that could easily have been the Garden of Eden. It was lush and green with juicy looking fruits sticking out from every corner. A clear stream flowed through the centre, demarcating the garden into two equal halves. Maybe I should call the nearest archaeologists and say: "Hey dude, I just found the garden of Eden in the Cashew bush" Every fibre of my being was again daring me to eat the apple Victor plucked and handed to me but my stomach was as usual only thinking of itself. Anyway, I thought, Eve could not resist, why would I? Or aren't we supposed to obey our parents?

I bit into the apple and chewed religiously like it was my lost heart I was trying to get into my body. My eyes followed Victor's index finger to the cup he was pointing at beside the stream. Goodness! I exclaimed under my breath. What manner of stream was this that did not want to be contaminated with dirty hands or cups? Whatever this place was, I wanted to have children and die here; and if this was a dream, I silently prayed to the spirit of dreams and nightmare that I did not want to end this part, even if it meant not waking up. I guess that spirit is really mean and heartless, because I had barely finished my drink of the purest kind of water that I had ever tasted before Victor suddenly grabbed my hand like I was a stubborn child and started leading me out of *Eden*.

"We have a lot to do" Was the casual explanation he gave for this inhuman wickedness. He tightened his grip on my hands as he led me through shrubs, on a relatively flattened parcel of land I had never seen in the forest. The prospects of this turning out to be a dream increased with each unnatural thing I saw. First, I saw a tiger, similar to the one that sent me overboard sanity the other day climbing a tree as swiftly as a monkey. Finally, if that was what this sudden halt meant, Victor brought me to a small body of water bounded by three gigantic trees so huge I could have sworn I could see across the Earth if atop one of them.

"Wear this" Victor said, before adding emphatically, "For your own good"

All this while, he was shoving in my frightened little hands a pair of spectacles that I had up till now neither seen sticking out of his hands or bulging in his pockets. Was this guy some sort of magician? I found my brain asking my heart. After a hesitation that I feared would drive Victor overboard with anger, I accepted the glasses and slipped them over my eyes. In no time at all, an incredibly bright light surfaced out of the river which Victor said was called 'The River' like creative names had gone out of fashion. Someone once remarked that scientists where good at making all these cool gizmos but terrible at naming them. For goodness sake, why would something that stores and plays thousands of songs simply be called 'Ipod?' Whatever happened to 'Music Impossible' or 'A thousand tracks' or even better, 'Hits +?' What I was trying to say was that whoever or whatever named this river could have easily done better. If I was in charge, I would call it 'LCD in the Ocean' or 'cinema H_2O'. Yeah, 'Cinema H_2O' would definitely have been super cool.

Like I was playing some sort of virtual game, the pictures I was seeing were high definition and appeared to be all around me like I was seeing the whole thing. Sorry, I mean, like I was actually there, and seeing it with my own eyes. I carried out a little experiment. I looked away from the river. When I was in Primary school, a friend of mine, Joshua, usually brought several puzzles. We would then spend hours after school cracking our small heads to get the solutions. I guess that's why a bit of me was watching out for those little, unnoticeable errors that usually came with movie productions. Somewhere in my mind, I was trying to make out why I would be drugged and placed in a movie set. Who said I was so scared of cameras? Alright, I know I was not making any sense. But would you if you were in my shoes? Seeing a video of this same school that appeared to have been shot several decades ago? And yet looked like the detailed product of a mega pixel camera? Presently, I could see an old, haggard woman near a coffin. She was writing something on a piece of paper. She kept on looking over her shoulders like she felt someone was watching. I tried to get a look at the tiny writings in red ink, but she kept on turning and covering it with her old, wrinkled hands. After about two minutes of careful writing, she suddenly stopped and looked back at the person I supposed she was trying to hide the writings from. She stared into the person's eyes coldly with black, very black eyes that had no whites, and shoved the wrinkled piece of paper she had been writing on in the person's face. I read. The person she was facing was me. She was showing me what she wrote. Nearby, Victor squeezed my hand like he was trying to prevent me from losing the pea sized amount of sanity I had left in my head. What she had penned down was written in a surprisingly beautiful handwriting and good English. Its words conjured what I conceived was some kind of prophecy. It said:

"There shall be five days of torture, and on the seventh day, a beast shall rise again"

"But...but, what then happens on the sixth day...today?" a question with such terrifying implications couldn't have been asked more simply.

"That's why we are here," the answer promised to be even simpler. "To find out"

Out of the blue, the answers started to flow. Some of them came from without, i.e. Victor; some from within-my puzzle cracker of a brain.

Victor was saying something about why we had to find the clues as to what would happen tomorrow or else...I was afraid of what the consequences he was suppressing were. I did not ask anyway. 'Let sleeping dogs lie' I convinced myself. Meanwhile, in my head, one question was reverberating. If the happenings of the past few days meant that the prophecy was about me, why did I get chosen? Why me?

Something outside my head was answering the question I thought only I heard.

"That is life for you." He was saying. No one gets consulted before they are given parents, a home; a life! It's the same reason why your name turns out to be Tayo; why Victor asks so many questions; why the sun comes in the afternoon to be replaced by the moon at night. It's just life. Plain and simple. I was already nodding my head to his philosophical mumblings when something checked in my mind. What did he say about Victor? Then I realised it wasn't what he had said, or not said about Victor, it was the way he referred to Victor in the third person. That was okay grammatically except for the fact that my eyes kept saying it was Victor who was talking. A puzzle cracker bulb lighted up in my mind. I had just gotten the first answer to one of the trillions of questions I have asked myself in the last couple of days. This guy beside me was not Victor. That was relieving. I took a deep breath.

The first place Pseudo-Victor led me to looked like a grave that had been excavated. Something about the scenery looked familiar, like I had seen this same grave in the past. I realised what it was. This was the very grave that old woman was writing on top in the movie Victor had just shown me. All of a sudden, I realised why there was so much sand on Pseudo-Victor. He had been digging! What exactly was in it for this guy? I found myself asking myself. After all I was the one involved in the prophecy (A smile formed on my face as I thought about this. I was beginning to sound like I actually believed all this fairy tale that was going on. These kinds of stuff never happened. Never!

Without the least hesitation, Victor, sorry, Pseudo-Victor jumped into the open grave. My right hand flew to my mouth to prevent it from screaming. Was this not a desecration of the resting place of the dead? Again, on cue, Pseudo-Victor answered my question like there was a loud microphone in his head amplifying my thoughts, so he could hear.

"If we should be worried about desecrations... Well too late, it has already happened."

Yeah, I thought. It happened the moment you jumped in there.

"What I am about to tell you is a ridiculous story" He started. What an irony, I thought. Someone that did not even exist was telling me that he was about to tell me a ridiculous story!

"I do not know if you guys know it, but hundreds of years ago, this school, or better still, the space the school now covers was a burial ground. When the first set of students were admitted about twenty years ago, the whole of this forest had not been cleared. By the way, have you ever wondered why students who visit the cashew bush are threatened to be expelled?"

Truthfully, I always thought it was absurd that the authorities even bordered about who ate cashew or not. Even after the principal was assured that after all the illicit visits to the forest, not even an ugly looking lizard was seen, not to talk of a menacing predator, they still insisted adamantly that we avoid the forest. I imagined this friend of mine was about to tie the ban to the old woman, but again that might sound equally queer. Maybe adults just hated it when kids were having too much fun!

Pseudo-Victor was still giving his own explanations. He was saying something about how the old woman's corpse was exhumed by some mischievous boys in the pioneer set of students in this school after they mistakenly stumbled across her burial site. He said this seriously vexed the spirit of the departed woman, who was reported to have been a witch in her lifetime. It was she who placed the curse. She, or should he say the boys (he added) were ultimately responsible for all that had happened to me in recent times. He immediately answered the question that was travelling from my head to my lips. The student who would be mainly affected by the curse could be deducted, he said, mathematically with the following formula: $x=2\sqrt{(3000-b)}$ where 'x' stood for the number on the admission list of the student, male or female and 'b' stood for the date of resumption from any holiday. This meant that sometimes, no one was chosen, or two pupils were chosen in quick succession, and when someone was 'privileged' (He laughed when he said this) to be chosen, his seven-day clock started clicking at any random time. By the way, he added again, the witch was a strong advocate of the supremacy of mathematics over every other subject.

Pseudo-Victor looked me in the eye and said to me, "What you should be bothered about is not the reason for an evil game played by a mischievous, evil woman; it is how the details add to your life...or end it that should scare you."

I too looked Pseudo-Victor in the eye and asked him just one question,

"Are you my guardian angel?" I said

22ⁿᵈ November

Yesterday, Victor False (or Pseudo-Victor) said Yesterday was the day of revelations and today was the day when the monster would rise again. Jokingly, I asked him what tomorrow was. He smiled when he noticed the sarcasm in my tone and said if this was a novel, tomorrow would be the epilogue, where it would be revealed who survived: The bad guy or the actor. He said I was the author of the book.

Yesterday, He and I darted from tree to tree, dug the ground to exhume rotten corpses like we were freaking archaeologists, recited incantations till lizards began to speak fluently in English, and spoke to the moon at night, all in a bid to solve the puzzle that Ogunsade Abacus (We even discovered the witch's names) left behind to entertain herself.

Yesterday, I watched a Cashew tree grow in a day. Guess what happened after that. Pseudo Victor made me eat twelve cashews in a row! "You have to finish it in a minute" was what he said cheekily. Anyway, I did eat. It put me into a deep sleep filled with nightmares. In the most memorable of those nightmares, I found myself on the tracks. I had to cover an unspecified distance in a minute. I imagine I did because when I finally reached the mysterious finish line that kept moving on its own at the end of the race, I met Evil game master (that was the witch's nickname) smiling coyly at me. She held my hands like she was in love and whispered into my ears words that chilled me to my bone marrow.

Yesterday, she said, "Run. Run like you have never done before because you must be pursued, and you must run. Just get to the light"

Today, when I woke up, I was sweating profusely. Pseudo Victor was nowhere to be found. I missed him like I have never missed anyone before. I missed him like I missed my bed once I woke up and had to go to class. I felt energised and light. I immediately sensed that I was feeling something else. It felt like someone was breathing on my neck. The person must have just returned from a sprint because he was breathing rapidly. I started to turn my neck so I could face Pseudo Victor when I told him to stop playing pranks. My motion was caught short when something slimy dropped on my forehead and began meandering towards my left eye. It was hot, heavy and slimy...like saliva.

Two things happened in flash.

One. I remembered how saliva dripped from the corners of my mouth when I was younger, and my mom placed beans and plantain in front of me.

Two. I have heard several times how one's life flashes before one when he was about to die. Mine just did placing particular emphasis on the last one week of my life. Pictures of Pseudo Victor and Yolly appeared in flashes before my eyes. They were talking so fast, I could barely make out what they were saying. I heard laughter coming out like words from the witch's mouth. I then saw my family in a picture, and friends by the roadside waving and me and then...I was running...

My heart pounded in a hundred thumps as I plunged blindly into the thick black forest in deep uncertainty. My five-foot physique got the trees thrusting hostile, sharp thorns in my face. As in a scornful hiss, the wind and the dry leaves conspired with my pursuer disclosing my locations. No one in my shoes will see such a hideous creature and challenge him to a duel. Hell no! Its charcoal black complexion and outstretched two-edged claws depicted a horrid picture from hell. A long, slender eye on its forehead easily earned it the name Cyclops, but another minute eye on its bare belly changed all that.

“☜⑨⑨✐✐ ☙⑥❶ ✋⑥☙③❺ ☙❧⓪⑤☙” It murmured in a strange language impossible to represent in written form. The wide chase continued, forcing me deeper and deeper into the forest. *Is this just a terrible nightmare, or is it true?* I asked myself praying the former was the case.

I could remember the stories Yolly, an ex-student had told me about cannibals in the school forest. Then I had laughed at him. He spoke of half men-half horses and talking trees among other tales I had tagged as ‘Yolly’s lullabies’ He had even shown a mild indignation when he sensed that his stories did not move me to fear.

☚⓪⑤⑤❧⑨🖹 ☙⓪⑤⑤❧⑨✐ A voice like roaring thunder a few inches behind me reminded me of my present predicament.

That was when I saw it.

A streak of God-sent light sparked some fire in my eyes. Perhaps, I would still live a little bit longer. Maybe I still have a chance with that pretty girl in my class. All I had to do was dash through...

"Aaa!" I was presently hoping, or better still praying I'd land in my mother's hands or at least in school, but of course that was a fantasy.

While running, the creeping roots of a tree got entangled with my legs, hence my sudden flight.

I landed with a great thump on my right elbow but that didn't matter a bit. At least not until I realized that standing up seemed a bit difficult, a little Herculean, convincingly impossible. I caught sight of a small girl in the school pinafore a few feet from my burial ground. She was last month reported as 'strangely dead' Rumours held that she committed suicide due to family problems she considered herself responsible for. It was now obvious that was a great deviation from the truth. Perhaps the same will be said about me. In my case, that the suicide was because of my inability to express my childish feelings to the person I dreamt of every night. Who said children don't fall in love?

He or rather, it, was now towering over me, certainly ready for dinner...ल☉⑤⑤∾⑨

I could see the headlines in 'The Daily Sun' November 22nd 1999.

"J.S.S 2 boy of F.G.C.L dies under mysterious circumstances." I shut my eyes in an attempt to say a last prayer, but instead just waited for my imminent division. The creature was unmistakably hungry judging by the drops of hot saliva that fell on my head. It lowered its trunk, gently. It smelt of death and I realized I was its prey as it revealed a pair of long fangs unlike any ever seen in any vampire movie. It was breathing hot air on my neck, which ironically, was really chilling.

It then got closer, and closer...

Then stopped.

Cyclops, or whatever it was tried covering its eyes as it stepped away from me. Suddenly it charged at me again, baring the fangs it wanted to drive into my skin. Again, it stopped. It appeared it was contemplating on what to do. I followed its eyes as it looked towards the sun.

"...just get to the light"

The words of Evil Game master struck me like a clock. I dragged myself towards the edge of the forest where the sun's rays could be felt more. My head hurt like hell. My heartbeat must have been something around 250 beats per second. The monster and I had been running for the last two hours nonstop. It, or sorry, I, took it round and round the forest. Under shrubs, above trees and even swam through that pure stream in the 'garden of Eden'. I guess it would have gotten way too contaminated for the next actor in this bizarre film I just ended, especially after that monster took a much-needed bath in it while chasing me around. Something hit me. I remembered that it actually forgot about pursuing me while it scrubbed itself in the stream. Goodness! What kind of flesh-eating monster did such a thing? Maybe it did not intend to kill me after all. Maybe this was merely a game planned by the evil game master.

I realised blood was flowing from somewhere near my eyes. I must have landed on my head when I fell. I was beginning to feel dizzy. Also, I was beginning to hear voices moving towards me. One of them sounded motherly. It appeared it was owned by someone who was prim and proper. Maybe my mum was finally coming to get me. Or maybe it was just my teachers.

I hoped they were not with their canes...

Epilogue

The three teachers who came to get me that day were led by Mrs. Olagunju. They told me a story I would not forget till death, not because it was in itself captivating, but because of the things it implied. Most prominent among this was the fact that during the entire episode, I felt somewhat comforted because something in the corner of my mind kept telling me that everything that was happening was a very twisted and protracted nightmare. However, by their testimony, it became obvious that the dreamy parts of it were simply due to the extreme exhaustion I must have experienced in addition to the concussions Chike inflicted on me.

They told me that they constituted a secret society in the school and had the onerous duty to ensure that every student that was chosen survived the task. The little girl, they said, could not be saved because she did not quite have the strength of character to survive the ordeal before they could intervene. Pseudo-Victor and the monster were actually a product of the spell the witch cast, so it appears she was not really intent on killing students. However, they said there was a catch to this. If the students who desecrated her grave were not brought to book, one student would end up dying once every ten years. Sharp mouthed teenager that I was, I bared my mind on what I perceived was their level of efficiency considering that they came after the whole thing ended like the Nigerian Police. Not at all, Mrs. Olagunju argued. When I was detained at the guardroom, the Gados had no idea what was going on even after asking several times. They were asked by Mrs. Olagunju to simply catch me and hold till the seven days elapsed. Because they were adamant on knowing what I did that was so hideous for them to break the normal protocols that determined their activities, Mrs. Olagunju had given them that story about the murder. She hoped that would keep them on their toes to make sure I did not escape. However, they mentioned that the witch never played fair in her dealings. She always had a joker placed to change how things turned out. Her joker this time around was Chike. He was hypnotized to do the things he did. Anyway, she added, the crimes he had done on his own volition were enough to have him expelled. As a matter of fact, she emphasized, he was no longer a student of this school. As Mrs Olagunju droned on and on to make sure I was not losing my sanity, I struggled to pinch myself awake, but the pangs of pain in possibly every tissue in my body made me know I could not be any more alert than I already was.

"Anyway" I breathed the word with what little strength I could muster.

"Thank God it's all over. At least I would not have to go through whatever the hell just happened to me again"

My pulse froze mid beat when I noticed Mrs Olagunju trying to force a smile.

"Em... well, technically..." I have never heard her search for words before.

Mr Akpan, who I just realised was beside her, placed his fat, brawny left hand on her shoulder and squeezed it gently.

"Yes, Tayo", she started, "This will never happen again".

THE END

Appendix

List of some of the Slangs and their meanings

(Arranged according to the order in which they appear)

Eyin: You (Plural form)

Abeg: Please

Shey: Used to emphasize a question

Yab: To insult or make fun of someone

Haba: Exclamatory remark

Igbotic: Has strong attributes of the Igbo tribe

Gbegborun: Yoruba word that means to gossip

Sheddars: Money

Sha: Might or Just

Jo or Joor: Yoruba word/slang for please

Shell: Make a grammatical blunder

Omo: Exclamatory remark or used to get someone's attention

Chop: Eat

Misyarn: To talk inappropriately.

Abi: Right?

Sef: Exclamatory remark

Baffs: Clothes

Gbese: Debt

Juju: Voodoo

THE MYSTERIOUS MATTER OF MALLAM MUSA'S MISSING MURANO

The weather outside was hot and dry with the humidity sucked out of the atmosphere to the very last drop of moisture, very much like the insides of Mallam Musa's mouth. He could not believe it had come to this. How could this people do this evil thing to him? His own family? But how could they be so callous?

He scanned the room carefully, narrowing his gaze so everyone he looked at knew just how serious the situation was. They were all crammed in the office of the Deputy Superintendent of Police (DSP) in the D-division of Biriniwa Local Government area of Jigawa State.

"So you're saying these are your suspects, eh?" the DSP, Mr. Shekarau said in fierce, fast flowing Hausa.

Musa would not be fooled by the hypocritical machismo. He knew the only reason this useless police man was listening to him was because Salah was fast approaching, and he was again hoping for a sizeable discount when he came to purchase ram for the celebration.

"So you think one of them did it, or they all worked together to commit the crime?" Shekarau asked again, simultaneously dusting a tattered notebook he had just rustled out from beneath a stack of files with the top one marked: 'Unsolved Cases'.

"I don't care if it was just one of these people or if they are all bloody accomplices, all I want is my property!" Musa was getting impatient. Something however tickled on his insides. He doubted if anyone else in the room understood what the word 'accomplice' meant. He prided himself to have been the first male among his peers as far as he could tell who made it as far as the final year of senior secondary school. Even though he flunked the final S.S.C.E exams, he always insisted that he refused to carry on to the university because he continuously was barraged by information that was contrary to his religious beliefs. He was after all, a devout, practicing Muslim man. That was one more thing he lied to himself about.

On hearing the word 'accomflice', Aisha immediately clutched her chest with the cup of her right palm. She could not believe her own husband was associating her with that word. Did it not refer to common criminals? How could he say such a thing? After all the nights he had spent lying on her bosom? After she had given him four children, all of whom were boys?

"Mallam, *haba*, Me your first wife?" She cooed softly to him, baring her teeth in astonishment.

Musa stole a glance at her before his gaze drifted off. He could not help but notice that as at current count, five of her teeth were already gold plated. He wondered what happened to the slim looking Fulani woman he married 20 years ago who had barely seen her first menses at the time, and screamed that witches were after her life the first time trickles of blood ran down her spotless leg. Those days, her legs were slim and long like the *Hadejia-Kafin Hausa River*. Now her tummy was bloated as if that nonsense doctor from her delivery last year had forgotten another baby in there. He never trusted the man anyway, with his funny accent and beardless chin. What kind of man shaved his beards anyway? He thought, stroking his impressive beards.

"Yes, you" Musa spat in her direction.

Ever since he purchased the Nissan Murano, making him the first man in the three compounds that constituted his extended family to buy a brand-new car, Aisha never failed to show her dislike of the car. At the time she had wanted him to give her money to go to Mecca for the sixth time, so she could come back and oppress her friends with some more gold teeth. He just hoped someday she would not come back with golden eyes when there were no more teeth to plate. Well, that would cause some trouble. How would she see properly when she was making him a bowl of *Tuwo Shinkafa*?

Musa shook his head at the foreboding feeling that one day, he might not get to eat the well-cooked *Tuwo Shinkafa* she was so great at preparing. His thoughts were interrupted by a familiar voice.

"*Yaro* Mu, let us think this thing over before we say things we should not say. Fighting with family and friends is like walking blindfolded in a maze of dark tunnels. It is impossible to trace back your steps once you set off."

Only one person in the world called Musa that. Just as he was the only one Musa knew who could come up with wisdom nuggets like that on his feet. Sanni had been Musa's closest friend for as long as he could remember. Since his mother died in childbirth, word had it that Musa's own mother had breast fed the boy as an infant as they were born at about the same time. They had rolled worn out tires down many dusty roads together, chased the smelly goats of Sheikh Abdulgafar round the market squares and even shared *Tsarance* partners in their youth.

Sanni sat cross-legged on a mat in the corner of the office with his back leaned against its dirty walls as he spoke. He was wearing his favourite white *Jalabia*, now brownish from repeated wear, so had no fears of the wall staining it. His square, muscular chins and soft eyes had made him the toast of many *yarinyas* in their heydays. Ever since Musa had bought that damn car, all had changed between them. He particularly remembered how Musa's eyes went from a mildly jaundiced yellow to fiery, sulfuric red when he joked about Musa's choice of car while they sat in it.

"Why did you not just buy a good Honda, like a respectable Hausa man?" He had said jokingly that day, referring to the automobile brand common among their ilk. Unfortunately, the joke was lost on his dear friend. He was always one to argue that White men had their own brand of black magic no matter what the literati said. Well, here was the proof. Musa had been bewitched by his own Murano!

Danjuma babbled something in a language only eight months old understand. He moved his small mouth in the direction of his mother's breasts but when it did not touch anything settled back to sleep. Mariam, Musa's youngest wife smiled lovingly at her child and then coyly in the direction of the DSP. The way her chest heaved quietly up and down, it was clear she was the only one other than Musbau (she insisted this was the boy's name, and not Danjuma) who had no inkling what on Earth she was doing in a police station. She had barely ever held a pencil in her entire life not to talk of learning to read. Hell, she might mistake it for something used to grind pepper if she saw one. Sometimes when Musa mused on her stark illiteracy, he wondered what attracted him to her, seeing how he believed someone with his wealth of knowledge of the ways of the *infidel* Westerners should marry someone of similarly impressive education. However, as he looked at her once again, the memories flooded back to him. Her thin lips and dimples, the way the shawl moved with her round, innocent breasts as she breathed; her fair, aquiline features and perfectly assembled dentition.

Musa suddenly snapped out of the reverie. She was as much of a suspect as anyone else in the room, and there was a simple reason for this. Barely a week after he had bought his beautiful, ash coloured, air-conditioned Nissan Murano with its leather interiors and buttons left, right and centre like a contraption that could take off into the air if you pressed the right ones- he had sneaked into Mariam's room and discovered something very shocking in her closet. She had always guarded this closet more secretly than the concubines of the Pope. Yes, he never for once believed any man could do without the warm embrace of a woman, but that was another story altogether.

Well, that day he found an impressive stack of two sachets of macaroni, his missing reddish-brown praying mat, a small pile of religious magazines and even a machete! He had a sudden epiphany. For someone who could not differentiate between the letters of the alphabet, it was strange what mental illness it was that empowered her to know which objects started with the letter 'M' and what magical spells they held over her. Another thought suddenly hit him like a quick blow. That was why she insisted her son's name was Musbau and not Danjuma, and more shockingly the way her demure disappeared as she screamed his name whenever they were getting to know each other better in his chambers! Well, he was not having any of that this time around. She had just touched the last 'M'.

He still had not gotten to play that 'aboki' song in his car. He wanted the ground to shake with a boom-boom whenever he drove by the thatched mud houses of some of his distant relatives. Unknown to him, his face was currently curling into a frown as he remembered that 'Izeprinze' or whatever it was that rapper called himself did not mention his name along with Dangote and his other favourite 'abokis' in the song. Musa was certain his name belonged to that list. Weren't his cows the fattest on this side of the Niger Delta? Did the herdsmen not confess that the milk they secreted from their udder were more delicious than fura de Nunu sold by Fulani hawkers. Just yesterday, he had given Usman, Aisha's teenage son some money to help him buy the CD and insisted the boy should not return home until he had gotten it. Well, Usman was yet to say anything about it. He was tapping his fingers anxiously on his laps as he leaned against the wall at the back of the room, sandwiched between Sanni and his step mother.

"Usman!" Musa barked at the boy and asked in Hausa. "Where is the thing I told you to buy, and where is my car?!"

"I don't know anything about that" Usman responded defensively, in a somewhat incoherent mixture of Hausa and English. He always wanted to impress his father with his mastery of the English language whenever he could but in his current state of confusion instinctively fell back to the language he spoke in his dreams. He wondered what had come over the man this time around. The last time he had seen his father this angry was when he asked for money for registration for JAMB examinations. His father angrily asked if it was because of his own university degree that the Emir of Ilorin had ordered for 5 of his fattest cows when Arsenal Football club played in the Champions League finals.

"What do you know about life?" Musa had said to the startled boy that day, in between a mouthful of cola nuts. "You better begin to learn the family trade. Who do you think will take care of my cattle when I'm gone?"

That ended the discussion that day, but somehow Musa knew the boy never forgave him for that. Secretly, the real reason he did not want the boy to advance in his studies was that he could not bear knowing that someone in his household was more learned than he was. He was after all the **head** of the house and had to be at the fore front of every aspect of their lives. It was enough that at 5 foot 10, the boy was already taller than him, even though not yet fully grown. He could not bear to have the boy become proud with knowledge also. Never! Who has ever heard of such a thing? Never!

"Mallam", after scribbling only God knows what in his small notebook for a couple of minutes, Shekarau suddenly looked up at Musa.

"You know how we like to be careful in our line of business, so we cannot make any arrests at the moment. We would have to carefully interview everyone one by one, to find out where they were between yesterday evening... that's when you saw the car last, not so?"

Musa nodded lazily, a slight headache announcing its presence as he did so. The question however continued to linger in his head as he suddenly started to ask himself when it was he saw the three-month-old car last...

****

"Listen, you this bloody civilian! You think I don't have better things to do with my time?"

A constable was screaming at an otherwise calm young man in the reception. Shekarau, in a move that defied his enormous potbelly, sprung from where he sat and trotted into the waiting area. The young policeman was seated behind the wooden reception desk with his legs crossed on a stool in front. He had an old newspaper in his hands. On the wall behind him was a green cardboard paper with the scribbled words:

The Police is your friend

"Sorry sir!" The constable jumped agilely to his feet, saluting the DSP at the same time.

"What is the problem here?" Shekarau drawled his words the way he knew *Ogas* had to so as to sound important.

"Sir, it is this man here", the constable said, pointing in the general direction of the bewildered man standing in his front with a perplexed look on his face.

"He said he wants to report a lost and found item, but..." The constable's words trailed off.

"***But***...?" Shekarau reinforced

"But", the constable's voice dropped to a shaky whisper

"...but he has refused to pay the *Listening* fee"

Shekarau almost jumped out of his skin when the stupid policeman said those words. He was not sure whether to jump across the desk and strangle the bastard to death for not being more discreet with their unwritten policies, or whether to run outside to buy a cup of *daddawa* and soak the man's lumpy eyes in them. He quickly looked around the room, beyond the stranger in their midst to see if anyone else around might have heard what was just said. Other than the three of them, no one else was there. His eyes finally settled on the Good Samaritan. He almost choked when he recognized the man.

"Sir", the man started, immediately wiping the subtle smirk off his face when he noticed that the DSP had recognized him.

"My name is Vincent. I run the ...em...em, adult English class on the outskirts of town. I'm sure you have heard about it"

"Go on!" Shekarau half yelped, half pleaded with a wave of his hand.

"Well, Mallam Musa is one of my students" His words were interrupted by a sudden short snicker from the constable who immediately started to cough violently when Shekarau sneered in his direction.

Who did they think they were fooling? The constable thought to himself. He knew all about the **Adult English Class** on the outskirts of town. For heck sake, he was a student there himself! Who wanted to face the wrath of their stiff *Sharia* laws by getting caught with beer in this their hypocritical town? Weirdly, he had once caught a disguised Sheik Danladi sipping a bottle or two in the place along with this his corrupt *oga*. Well, he made a quick resolution to play along. This was after all Nigeria. Nothing was as it was meant to be.

"...It appears Mallam was ...em, really tired after last night's session" Vincent continued his tale unperturbed, dressed in a blue *bubban riga*, brown leather palm sandals and white skullcap. "I saw him walk past his new car as he chartered a commercial motorcycle, got on it with his hands in the air, and ordered the rider to start moving"

"Wait", Shekarau interrupted. "What do you mean by his hands in the air?" He asked.

Vincent lifted both his hands and placed them on an invisible steering wheel above his head that he turned it from side to side, the furrows on his forehead deepening as he concentrated on what he was doing.

"Sir, it would appear that Mallam Musa drove only his car keys back home!"

"Hmm..." Shekarau sighed, scratching his head. How strange it was that the first case to be solved in this police station since he was appointed DSP 3 years ago should pass by very quickly.

At this rate, he would become a commissioner in no time at all. He definitely had a way with mysteries.

THE END

Glossary

- **Aboki**- Meaning friend in Hausa. The context in which it is used refers to a song by favourite Nigerian rapper, 'Iceprince Zamani' called Aboki

- **Bubban riga**- A large flowing gown worn by Hausa men.

- **Daddawa**- Local pepper source

- **Fura de nunu**- Freshly expressed cow milk to which ground millet has been added.

- **Haba**- Slang used to express emotion or exclamation.

- **Hadejia Kafin** Hausa river- A river in Jigawa state, Nigeria that flows from west to east.

- **Infidel**- Unbeliever

- **Jalabia**- A long flowing robe worn by Hausa men

- **Oga**- Boss or superior

- **Sharia**- Islamic law

- **Tsanrance**: Institutionalized practice where boys and girls are allowed to sleep together, fondling and petting each other but without penetrative sexual intercourse

- **Tuwo Shinkafa**- Thick rice pudding

- **Yarinya**- A girl
- **Yaro**- A boy

THE GROWTH

I eased myself gently into the old, brown sofa in the sitting room, my hands on my sore back. My dirty white eyes settled on the aged brown clock hanging obediently on the wall. The seconds hand moved round and round but did not return my stare. It just was not interested in my state of affairs. All that occupied it was what clocks were made to do- to tick and to tock. I realized I had drifted into a reverie where I could be anything I wanted to be- A swallowtail butterfly with my forked hind wings spattered with bold, dark colours. I would flutter my wings gracefully as I sipped nectar from plant to plant without a care in the world. I remember watching tons of documentaries as a child, but none captured my imagination like the one that taught me all I still know about butterflies. Perhaps I could be something more real- human even. Maybe I would be a very important lady like our pastor's wife. She seemed to always have a smile on her face as she listened attentively whenever her heartthrob was on the stage leading people to heaven. One day I stumbled onto a conversation between Sisters Rose and Loveth where they openly discussed pastor's obviously well-known libido and sex escapades. I was shocked they could discuss such a delicate matter in a bus over the noisy sounds of Lagos. They were shocked I did not already know about it, either from hearsay or personal experience. Loveth started off saying something that sounded like "...but he never come jam fine geh like you?"

Something squeezes inside me whenever I recollect the way her voice dropped like a heavy sac of rice as she took in my unkempt appearance. Something squeezed me back to reality as I tried to rub off an ache in my lower back.

Everything hurt! Walking, sitting... defecating. I felt fat and ugly. Instinctively, my right hand went to my face to brush aside wisps of hair from my forehead. Damola, my late husband, always said my forehead was one of my beautiful features.

'Damo' as I fondly called him was my sunshine. He was the shooting star in my eerie black skies lighting my world with his brightness. Tofu tasted like fried meat if he fed me. His touch made me blazing hot when it was cold outside. He wrapped me in a warmth of kind words whenever rain beat me, and I shivered in his father's shed like a fly caught in an avalanche. The first day he spoke to me I was convinced father Francis' sermon every Sunday about the love of God had to be true. Think of it- I was the first female child of my father's battalion of 18 children to go as far as JSS3. The first time my father hugged me was when he saw my WAEC result. That day he called me doctor. God! Warm blood instantly coursed through my veins! I realized I was blushing now as I remembered how Damo also made warm blood engorge my thighs and pelvis with his sneaky little fingers. My dad's smile however was not warm when he learnt that his 17-year-old baby girl was herself about to become a mother. Worse still, the bastard child belonged to a child whose family had a tradition of untimely deaths. One decade, three pregnancies and a very eventful lifetime after and I was still convinced it was I who killed my father. Well, of course the short doctor who spoke a bit too fast assured us he died from natural courses. He mentioned something like a 'miocarda infaction' that day. When mama's lower lip stooped helplessly forward as she wondered why papa had to die "in fact" he quickly quipped that it was a heart attack.

I just stood transfixed besides papa's favourite wooden stool as I stared into his lifeless, wide eyed face. He stared back without blinking at me. I thought I heard him ask why I had stolen his heart and stitched a heartache into it with my baby's tiny fingers.

I would be lying if I said getting married to Damola was such a terrible idea. On the contrary our years together were memorable in a good way. He was acutely aware that getting pregnant was the reason I had to drop out of school. He seemed to have literally died trying to fix that. He worked none stop from dawn to dusk. If there was money to be made, Damola's name always came up as the go to guy. He painted, traded, transported, farmed, and even danced for money! One day at the ripe age of 35 he simply slumped while making a wooden chair for our lousy next door neighbours. I think he was simply tired of asking God why life had to be so hard. That was the last day I prayed.

As two bouts of sorrow started to descend gingerly on me like feathers floating in the wind, I felt a short, painful kick in my stomach. I suddenly had an overpowering need to dip my two hands underneath my skirt and pull it out; to watch its lifeless body dangle by a bloody cord attached to my innards; to strangle its treacherous little neck till the very life squished out of it. I started thinking up all the ways to kill a baby. If I had the money for an abortion I would have gotten one once I knew I was pregnant. To hell with pastor's talks about it being murder! At least we now know he is not a saint himself. Which one was a more terrible sin, adultery or abortion? When the thought started to creep in that I was not likely to win that argument I went back to thinking of all the ways to kill a baby. Maybe I would take the pains to deliver it then boil its shiny bald head in hot oil. But of course, I was no stranger to labour and unsure if this particular baby was worth the stress. Or should I simply thrust my kitchen knife into my abdomen hoping to hit its tiny chest heaving up and down quietly in my womb. But of course, I would be killing myself in the process. Anyway, the knife was as dull as my father's fifth wife- the Hausa one he brought back from his journey to Zaria. What was her name again? Umar or something like that. Lord!!! I just felt like strangling a baby right now!

Jesus! How did it come to this? I remember that miserably hot afternoon as clearly as my name. I had just gotten to Mama Nkechi's house where after what felt like an intense interrogation, she lent me the twenty thousand naira for my daughter's school fees. She spat, she cursed, and she made me swear to Ahmadioha, Ogun and every other indigenous god she was acquainted with. All I could think of was giving Simi, my 14-year-old daughter the chance I threw away. If it meant a few incantations here and there, then by Jove I would do it. Mama Nkechi had barely tossed the money I wanted in my face and shut her gate against me when I noticed a man walking towards me. He was an ugly, squatty man with garlic breath asking for direction to a place that I currently cannot remember. He was dressed casually in checked blue shirt and chinos trousers with a well-polished leather palm slippers. I sort of remember that he unfolded a piece of paper from his left back pocket as if to show me a map of the place he was going. A putrid powdery smell hit my nostrils like a Tyson punch. Next thing I knew I was in a haze; half awake, half asleep. It felt like my mind had been closed in a jar and thrown down an abyss. I felt myself spinning and spinning while the treacherous hands of something from Hades own garden stretched out to receive me.

When I came to, I felt something heavy holding me down. As my eyes got accustomed to the dim light around me, I realized two heavy, sweaty men were holding me down while a third one was on top of me. A black candle burned sparingly in the corner. I noticed what looked like egg shells and blood-stained cat eyes surrounding the candle. I remember the man with the garlic breath as he rammed in and out of me. He was mumbling something in a language I did not know. I remember hoping to die. Someone squeaked behind me. I could have sworn it sounded like a female.

"Bamuza, I no get time. Make we do wetin we come do comot from here"

I almost fractured my cervical spine as my neck spun around to see who just spoke. Pardon me. I knew who just spoke. I just had to see her face as she said those hideous things. I knew the stale smell of her orange wrapper if I smelled it from the other end of town. It was the one with her dead mother's face looking sternly in a perpetual scowl. I took in her dirty well-worn Dunlop slippers sticking into my hair. Her off white blouse revealed two sagging, wrinkled breasts as she leaned forward as if to allow me to see her clearly.

Mama Nkechi spat in my face.

Gazillion thoughts swirled in my head all at once. They hit every side of my skull as my heart raced like a turbojet. What did this all mean and what did I do to qualify for it. Did I still owe her any money before today? I thought of a certain three thousand naira I borrowed when I and the kids went hungry for 3 days. But immediately I remembered I paid it back after I donated blood at the private laboratory down our street. Did I offend her in any way? Was she just trying to make money off my *chi*? Was that even wise- I mean, she knew the cards life had dealt me thus far. Was there any good in my blood?

When the three men were done having their way with me, Mama Nkechi's hands brushed my nostrils with that same pungent, powdery substance. I woke up the next day in front of my house. Simi was rubbing my right shoulder desperately.

"Mummy, mummy!!!"

Her teary eyes were three quarter dead frightened, one quarter sad. I spent the next two days having as many warm baths as possible before I summoned the courage to go to Mama Nkechi's house. I had to look her eyeball to eyeball, woman to woman and ask her why. I met a 'To let' sign on her gate with an obviously empty house. I wished I knew where her divorced husband was with the children she never even spoke about. It occurred to me that this was the sort of thing you reported to the police, but I just did not have the transport money to spare. The last three hundred naira with me was budgeted for feeding for the next two weeks. No one ever seemed eager to buy the provisions I had to sell. It was like there was a sign atop my kiosk I could not see. I bet it read: "Death, sadness, stolen dreams."

Or should I call Damo's mother? Could she be of any assistance? Would she even pick my call? She vowed to never speak to me the day we buried Damola. I just felt tired of asking *'why me?'* I was simply tired of being tired.

I remember the doctor telling me three months later that I had two things growing inside me: one a baby, the other a virus. He just sat there in his white overcoat, cheap tie and smug face and stole what remained of my future with his words. I could swear he bit his tongue when he mentioned that the ideal thing in this situation would have been to terminate the baby but that it was against his faith. He went on and on switching from grim news breaker to motivational speaker, but all his words did was to sear the fresh wounds along the edges of my heart. The baby, he reiterated was the better half of the story- the more worrisome thing was that I would need to be on drugs for the rest of what remained of my pathetic life- nay sanity. Luckily, he added, like I had any of that assigned to me, the drugs were provided freely by an agency whose name I was too distraught to commit to memory.

Finally, I remember that this innocent child was half evil, yet half me; a mischievous canvas painted from the colours of fate and happenstance but smudged with an ugly strip of man's inhumanity to man. This child was the unknowing character called to play his part in a play he did not write. So each day I remember all the things I hate, I remember that one thing none of us ever had any power over was when to be born; how to be born. It suddenly occurs to me that as long as life breathes, love can exist, and even dark colours can paint beautiful pictures. For some insanely strange reason, I placed my right palm over my abdomen and somehow knew that I had a new beginning before me. Very different, very painful but new nonetheless- and I made up my mind to take in all the colours life threw my way.

MADIBA'S MOLE

I am the innocuous onlooker on the bridge of his nose, a keen witness to his life and times. I was there when at 12 his father, Nkosi Mphakanyiswa breathed his last and King Jongintaba Dalindyebo wiped the tears streaming down beside me and said I was now his, and he, mine. I shuddered with the rest of his nose when our primary school teacher, without our consent, concluded Rolihlahla was too much of a mouthful and christened him Nelson. Till now the thought tickles me, did that make me a Christian mole?

Even when I was not clearly visible, I was always there for Nelson under the surface, an unspoken but vivacious part of his identity. I bobbed up and down on his face as we fought injustice at Fort Hare, spoke for the down trodden, and gave blood, tears and years whenever prejudice reared its unsightly head. We stayed up all night, eyes glued to lengthy legal letters, as he struggled through his articles at Witkin, Eidelman and Sidelsky.

I swear I lost a heartbeat when I saw Evelyn. She radiated a peace I had never experienced in her dazzling white nurse uniform. I too was drawn to her brilliant eyes and soft skin. I found myself subconsciously searching for a mole on her face... ok a small blackhead? Dimple? Any spot at all? My God! She was flawless!

It is 2016. The apartheid war has been fought and won (Or has it?). We have ruled our dear nation and left an eternal legacy behind. I have loved, lost and loved again. Now I rest silently on Rolihlahla's skeletal face, but we are not at peace. Our people have left the enemy at the gate and cut up our brothers at home... like amnesiac bloodletting butchers.

THE LETTER MY SHOE SENT ME

I step out of our house with my hands in my pockets. For some strange reason I feel surprisingly good about myself, recent circumstances notwithstanding. Maybe it is just the feel of the sun's warmth on my skin. That thought makes me smile. In some poems, writers describe the sun and moon with such embellished language, making them out to be something more than the celestial bodies that they are. Well, who am I to discredit the life work of another? We all have to find a way to make a living. From the corner of my eyes, I can see my mum peeking at me from behind our woollen curtains with bewildered suspicion. I do not blame her anyway, she just does not understand. A quick 5 minutes trot and I am already outside Medium housing estate, Ogba, waving to an oncoming public bus to pick me up. The driver pulls up beside me James Bond style, barely missing an opportunity to crush my right foot. I instinctively jump back in fright. The bare-chested bus conductor rears his square faced head from inside the vehicle uninterested in the shock on my face.

"Ikeja unda brige, 200 Naira! Enter with ya change, I no be CBN" He spits in pidgin English, his muscular right arms latching onto the roof of the vehicle- a little trick most likely taught in whatever

school they learn their art, to keep them from tipping over as their buses dribble recklessly through the dense Lagos traffic. I stumble into the vehicle, feebly noticing the steep tribal marks etched on either side of the bus conductor's face. It has been said that people with such tribal marks are particularly wicked. Who comes up with such theories anyway? Are they true?

"*Go on souun*" He screams at the driver who automatically steers the bus back into a sea of oncoming vehicles. One Toyota Camry misses colliding with our bus by a hair's breadth. Its driver peeps out his window, scowling in our direction. Our driver replies by fanning out his right hands at the man in a traditional symbolic expletive.

"*Waka! Ya mama yansh!*" He says, insulting the man's mother's derriere for no particular reason. Who comes up with these insults anyway?

By now I am more comfortably seated in the 3rd row of seats near the window, on the driver's side. I quietly take in the faces of the people around me. To my right is a slim, fair complexioned lady- I guess of the Ibo tribe- she is dressed very brightly in body hugging green leggings and tucked in flowery, orange shirt. A black leather bag is propped up on her left elbow, brazenly foraying into my own elbow room. A somnolent elderly man lets his head droop onto the shoulder of a brutish looking, squat chap in front of me. The latter looks with disgust at the face of the old man, mutters something under his breath, and then looks at his watch again. It is about 8.30 am. Most of the passengers look eager to get to work so they can continue the rat race that defines their lives. I graduated from the University of Ife just 2 months ago with a degree in Economics myself. I really have no idea what to do next with my life. Will a master's degree help bolster up my dim second class lower grade? A postgraduate degree outside the country would have been the way to go, but unless some white man's scholarship sends me there, it is unlikely I can afford the ridiculously high tuition fees. Daddy's business is barely trudging on in this rather depressing economic climate and his only focus now is saving enough money to send Segun, my younger brother, to a 'proper law school', as he puts it. Segun is the one with the big words and curious expression. He is the only person I have ever known who looks forward to vacation days, not for the sheer thrill of not having to study but so he can gingerly place his report card in daddy's brawny hands and watch as his face lights up with joy. To my father, I am like a cloud of smoke before the eyes of a drunken man that looks like an exciting object at first, but in a brief moment of clarity the man sees the object for what it truly is- a lacklustre cloud of smoke. Full stop.

I get dragged out of my reverie when I perceive the jaundiced eyes of the conductor staring at me. His greasy right hand is almost in my mouth.

"*I go beg u to give me ya money?*" He quizzes in disgust.

I quickly rummage through my pocket to bring out the dirty Naira notes in it. I only have 500 naira bills with me. I squeeze one into his hand.

"*Wetin I talk about change? You be mumu?*" He questions my IQ insolently.

My lips part to defend myself against his foul mouth but the words refuse to come out.

"*Haba now! Wetin? No be change dey your hand so?* I retort. Or think I say.

It does not take long to remember that no one hears me now. Ripples of despair descend to settle permanently in my mind. I feel like a man buried alive in a transparent coffin; screaming, banging, thrashing his legs about wildly to hopefully attract enough attention to get saved. But everyone just looks him in the face and walk away wordlessly like zombies who do not speak his language. *Nobody speaks my language these days. No one understands silence.*

In a little under 90 minutes we arrive in Ikeja. As everyone disembarks from the bus, I tap the conductor's shoulder from behind in a bid to collect the change he owes me. He shrugs off my hand without looking back and briskly walks towards a horde of pedestrians on the other side of the road.

"Ogba, Ogba!!" He screams at them. *"No need for full load, we dey comot now!"* He lies.

An action hero in a Japanese movie once said that there is no cowardice in accepting when you have been beaten. He must have been talking about this moment. My hands go back into my pockets as I set off for my final destination, my eyes fixed on the road in front of me. It does not feel so good this time around.

Several newspaper vendors have crammed wooden benches in every conceivable space under the bridge I am currently walking under. My eyes catch a glimpse of the headlines on one of the popular dailies.

"The Nigerian Army slaughters scores of Boko Haram Operatives!" The subheading beneath the picture of a ragtag group of soldiers read: "It was a swift and decisive victory, reports army general"

I scoff. These media people make me laugh. I do not know who to believe. Just last night, one of the electronic media houses reported that the same extremist group was gaining more grounds in the North East, Now this? Ultimately news is what the newspaper editor says it is- and the editor hears what his bankrollers allow him to.

These things occupy my mind so keenly that I am totally absent minded as I arrive at the hospital-Lagos state University Teaching hospital, pay my consultation fees and wait to be called upon by the overweight nurse with too much red lipstick, who shuffles about- surprisingly quickly for her weight- in immaculate white uniform.

"Oluwagbotemi Adebayo!"

Ni bo iyen ri lo ba yi? She asks about my whereabouts rhetorically in fluent Yoruba.

"Oluwagbotemi Adebayo!!"

She sneers in my direction when I jump up and point me towards the consultation room as she picks up my hospital folder from a plastic desk.

An ocean of curious eyes bore into me as I step into the room. A balding man with astonishingly round cheeks motions for me to seat down facing him. He is flanked by all sides by at least a dozen medical students. I eerily feel like a claustrophobic jar of honey in a room filled with bees. A tall and slim doctor appears from nowhere at my side. He is the Hausa doctor who scheduled me for today's visit. He is most likely a junior doctor and Mr. 'Roundface', whose self-satisfied smug expression I desperately want to rub off with a back-hand slap, is perhaps his boss.

"Sir this is the patient I discussed with you on the phone" The slim doctor says in a quirky, heavy, northern accent.

"Oh, I see" comes the response. The consultant then spends the next few minutes reading the ineligible-to me at least- cursive writing of his subordinate in my file. Occasionally he would look up from the notes and into my face, as if to corroborate what was written, utter an "hmm" or "aha!" and get back to what he is reading. I feel like a medallion being marketed to a meticulous pirate. Or am I dying?

"Have you requested for an MRI?" The consultant asks. The Hausa doctor who is first taken aback by the question begins to build up an excuse of how the machine is not working and mentions something about the cost of the test and how I cannot afford it. It is surprising my well pressed second-hand clothes have given me away so easily.

The senior doctor, half-excited, half-irritable keeps on firing questions at the poor junior doctor in rapid quips.

"Anything remarkable in his family and drug history?"

"Any other deficits"

"Any features suggestive of depression"

"Hope you were able to elicit a psychosocial stressor" (I figure this is the terrible thing that must have happened to me that the doctor kept on asking me about 2 weeks ago, to which I could only shake my head. Maybe I did not answer because he was asking the wrong question. Maybe he was asking the wrong person.

"I imagine you documented how exactly you two communicated?" The senior doctor asks all this while animatedly reading the file. His face seems to shine brighter with every word.

"Good. At least you had the common sense to get an '*otorino...*' (The rest of the word is lost on my non-medical ears) consult.

"Anyway, what are your differentials?" Something about the way the doctor put it makes it sound like a trick question. Hopefully they are about to discuss exactly what they think is wrong with me. Thus far, I felt like the major actor in a play I had not rehearsed for. I listen more intently. The least item I should take out of this enchanting encounter is an idea of what the hell is wrong with me.

"I think it could be hysteria," He starts, but sensing some discomfort in his boss, the slim doctor quickly adds, "But more likely some sort of conversion disorder"

"Exactly!" The consultant booms. I can swear a smile is playing around his lips as he says this.

"Dr. Musa, we need to tie this thing up very, very neatly. This is very reportable." He is rubbing his chubby hands excitedly by now. One petite, bespectacled student rushes forward to look at me more intently. Something about the diagnosis has definitely piqued her interest. I guess she is the *'effico'* of the class-the extra studious student. This makes my mind quickly drift to Segun. I suddenly feel like the Gulf of Alaska-happy and sad at the same time.

At the moment Dr. Musa is writing a letter for me. He is saying something about a test, an EEG that I have to do which is not available in their centre. The senior doctor continues where he stopped and is explaining their need to do more extensive tests, and how I am going to be okay eventually, and how they would prescribe some drugs for me in the meantime.

Their words fall through the tunnels of my ears but do not register a thing. All I can think about is how much simpler things were when I was a child and how much the world has changed with the very dictates of nature twisted on its hinges. My mind is stuck on how I was always somewhat dismissive of Segun no matter how nice he was to me. Truth is I once envied his intellect. Now, I am not so sure if all that will amount to anything. All I can think about are immense opportunities and truncated aspirations; parental expectations and broken dreams and I wonder if I should be thinking so hard at all.

The Lagos sun is at its fiercest when I get home. It is a huge relief stepping into the house as my eyes try to adjust to the change in ambient light. Faustin, our Congolese house help tries his best to catch my eyes as he bids me welcome. I try my best to hide the belligerent disgust in them as I storm into my room. For goodness sake! What has this house help gotten Segun into? The boy is just some months over fourteen and in his penultimate year in the secondary school. How long has this gone on for? I do a quick mental math to try to figure this out. Faustin has been with us for at least 7 years now. But then, Segun is barely pubertal. Does he even know what an erection feels like? Wait, when did I first learn about sex myself? These thoughts jar in my head like particles in the Hadron Collider. It was exactly 3 weeks ago when I walked in on both of them in the sitting room in the middle of the night. My parents travelled for the burial ceremony of an old uncle, so I felt care of the house was my responsibility. It thus felt natural that I stopped both of them from watching movies late into the night. Unfortunately, it turned out the loud television set was simply a decoy. I caught both of them frolicking in the nude on the centre couch. My catholic eyes could not comprehend what I was seeing. That scene literally took the breath out of me. Then my voice.

My parents first thought I was on to an annoying prank when they noticed I had literally stopped talking. Daddy was the first to lose his temper over the matter.

"Have you finally gone mad?!" He asked, hopefully rhetorically. I had no idea I had that to look forward to.

My mum immediately whiskered me into her room and bore into my eyes sympathetically. She noticed I was sobbing hysterically and saw how widely I was opening my mouth in a desperate attempt to speak. Everything else worked. I could hear everyone else perfectly and had no loss of motor function. My eyesight was perfect. It was just words that had been knocked out of my throat in one fateful jab. I had no idea how much words meant to me before that day.

Presently I am lying on my side in the room and looking in the direction of my black leather shoes, stacked under the plastic table in the corner. These shoes have served me nonstop for the last 3 years. How ironic that it was my favourite uncle, the one who died recently, that gave them to me as a gift on my 18th birthday. A thought occurs to me and it makes me chuckle. If those shoes were to write a letter to me, what would they say?

Strangely, I realize I am already hunched over my desk in a little over 2 strides. I am about to do something I have never ever done before- write a poem or write anything fictional at all of my own volition!

The letter my shoe sent me

I start, rather unsure how these things should start at all. Well this is about a letter my shoe sent me; I might as well start this way.

Was just a few words long

Hahahahahaaaa, I laugh to myself. It has to be a short letter. How many English words do I know anyway?

Use me. Clean me. Keep me.

I pause here. Something tells me the next line has to rhyme with something else I have written, somehow.

Yet its memory lingers on.

"Ladies and gentlemen, behold my first stanza" I say out loud, unafraid that someone might wonder if Daddy's prophesy of my inherent madness has actually come true- I no longer have words to speak, so there is really no reason to fear. The drugs I was prescribed today lay untouched at the edge of the table. Maybe I would start them tomorrow; maybe I would not touch them at all.

With every line comes an empowering feeling that I have found my voice. It makes me feel astoundingly alive and free; liberated and unhinged, like all the problems in the world cannot stop me from being happy.

On the dot of 55 minutes from where I started, I place the last full stop in my first poem. I read it once more from start to finish, making sure I have not missed any misspells or errors.

The letter my shoe sent me
was just a few words long
'Use me. Clean me. Keep me'
Yet its memory lingers on.
The letter my shoe sent me
was clear, concise and simple,
though written in faint ink
the mark it made remains indelible.
The letter my shoe sent me
is like one I myself once wrote
to my teacher, lean and mean,
a tiny scribbled note.
The letter my shoe sent me
was just three words long,
polish not punish,

so its memory lingers on...

I lay back on my bed with an accomplished smirk on my face as I recite the words in my head. Something nags on in my mind about how 'my shoe' in this poem is a metaphor for something else, someone else even. But this is supposed to be a good moment, so I empty my mind of these uncertainties. Poets must feel about their poems the same thing I feel for food. Everything I cook tastes excellent on my palate no matter what anybody says. Maybe it is because there is something personal about what you are involved in making. No wonder a popular maxim in Nigerian Pidgin English says that *"Monkey no fine but him mama like am"*- No matter how ugly a monkey is, its mother loves it.

Possibly I'd send this one in for one of these popular awards, Caine or even Nobel Prize. Who cares how these things get judged, this is a really good poem. I chuckle once more.

"Nice" I say.

It suddenly strikes me that I have just spoken...out loud.

So I try again to rule out any fluke.

"Very nice" I say again.

Nothing births sadness like the unspoken words in silence; nothing is more forlorn than the wretched soul that has lost its voice.

It feels good to speak and be heard, once more. I have so much to say.

EUTHANASIA

Two men stared each other down in the arid heat of Birnin-Gwari, Kaduna. They stood like impromptu statues on the alleyway sandwiched between the city mosque and the general hospital, a dreary metaphor of the unfolding events. The younger man maintained a resolute icy stare as his finger wrapped around the trigger of a Ruger LC9. His fine features, designer clothes and muscular build cut a picture of a life well lived. His father stood shakily at the other end of the barrel dazed and confused. A gentle Sahara breeze momentarily caressed his dry skin, pressing his *Jalabia* against his thin legs before quickly blowing away – even the wind would rather not be a part of this, the man thought to himself.

"Musa, *don Allah*". Viscous tears welled up in his father's eyes as he begged for his life in the name of their God. He raised both hands in surrender, his calloused palms facing his first and most loved child, a witness to the sacrifices he had made for his children.

"What is going on? What have I done?" The old man pleaded. The words he left unsaid hung heavily in the air like a putrid smell.

Musa squeezed the trigger in two quick successions. He pumped two 9mm rounds into his father's torso.

The old man fell to the ground like a bag of beans, his wrinkled face contorted in a weighty mixture of shock and anguish. Is this how it all ended for him? All those years of toiling on his benefactor's farm in Saudi Arabia, just so he could provide the kind of life for his children he could only have dreamt of as an unkempt *Almajiri* boy growing up in the city of Kano. Is this what it all came to?

Musa pressed the nozzle of his pistol against his own temple.

As he started to pull the trigger, a sudden epiphany hit him. Most people opine that the important question was how to die. Was it better to watch your flesh dry out on the bones underneath as some strange illness tore at you from the inside? Was it better to die in old age surrounded by family who you could neither see, hold or hear clearly as each of your bodily functions raced against each other to see which one failed first? Or was dying in a battle on foreign soil, dignified and courageous, as some random infidel cut your throat with a dagger more appealing? Now that his time had come, he realized it was the why that counted. '**Why**' is the ultimate question.

Just that in this case the answer was unclear. All he could think about were the voices in his head. They went on and on like a chatter of monkeys. Cheerless, imposing monkeys.

"You need to kill your father" they said.

"He will become the antichrist and burn in hell"

"He will drag you and everyone into its bleary furnace"

"Do you see the way the community look up to him because of his integrity and piety? He will lead them astray and cause gnashing of teeth on all sides"

"Do it! Do it" they thundered.

As incoherent as they sounded, the voices were clear about what he needed to do. They were lucid about who he needed to do it to.

Bright lights flashed in his eyes as the gun powder exploded. Musa felt a gentle wave of peace settling in his heart. The kind of peace that could only have been born of mercy- mercy like he showed his father.

Maybe he will finally be free this time around. Pastor Gabriel's prayers did not save him. He knew how fond the pastor was of him. He was the child of a stout Muslim who had found their Lord, a poster boy for all things bright and beautiful in the evangelism department of Deliverance Christian Ministries. When Musa began to grapple with voices in his head, the pastor thought it was a piece of cake. This was the devil trying to take back what he lost. So, he prayed and prayed, one fire and brimstone session after another but nothing changed. Clocks chimed, seasons passed, and Musa got more withdrawn and dark.

Dr. Danjuma's pills were not of much benefit either. His pot belly bobbed and bobbed in his clinic as he tried to convince Musa's father that he was on top of the matter. His medical certificate and an array of carefully selected pictures strategically placed around the office bore testament to his medical ingenuity. In one of the pictures, he was firmly shaking the erstwhile minister of health, Dr. Waheed Hussein, as he peered cheerfully into the camera. In another, his shiny white coat stood in contrast to the tattered clothes of the horde of children of a nearby village flustered around the man, with his fancy words and stethoscope.

Fluoxetine, Sertaline, quetiapine; the names of the pills the pharmacist thrust into Musa's hands got more amusing with each clinic visit yet his demons almost seemed angrier as they waited for him outside the walls of the decrepit hospital. The hospital that now stood beside him, a reluctant witness to a demonstration of mercy.

Perhaps this time the voices that tormented him will finally be usurped by quiet. More so, if there was the slightest chance they were correct, he had saved his father from troubles unheard of. He had saved a dying world from a quick and horrendous ending. But of course, this world was rather keen on some form of ending with the desperation with which man depletes earth's resources and pollutes its waters. Anyway, he had played his part.

Musa's last glimpse was of his father lying in a puddle of his own blood, an aghast stare eternally etched on his face. As his lungs sucked in their last breath, he prayed for the soul of his father, and his own wretched being. He hoped his father would forgive him wherever it was people went after this place. After all, they were family, and the sweetness therein was that family forgave each other.

NOSTALGIA

"I remember the first time I was in love It was all the way back in 1997 I stole my mama's cell phone, yes, and I was turning it up..."

The Danish songstress' awkward voice tickled my ears as I walked uphill on Clarkegrove road, Sheffield. I sniffed in deeply to capture a whiff of the autumn sunset flowers that dotted Shirley's living room. From the angle of my left eye I could make out the wrinkled face of the octogenarian. She was always there when I walked by, peering from behind the curtains, monitoring my every move. I wish she would simply grow up. So much has happened over the last 40 years. I wonder why she was still stuck in the past.

She was not alone. I was getting increasingly thankful my eyesight and hearing was diminishing by the day because I was simply getting sick and tired of the surreptitious glances and whispers that trailed my evening walks.

"Oh my God! Isn't that the guy on grandpa's poster? The foo..." A cherry faced boy tried to wriggle free from his nana's clasp on his mouth as they walked past on the opposite sidewalk.

I suddenly wished those defenders hit my head harder all those years. I was getting sick of this.

By now I was just halfway up the street. It felt like I had walked for a generation already. If only my left knee would cooperate with me. Well, to be honest, I was able to get out of bed 5 minutes faster today. That was my personal best for the past few months. The Indian GP I consulted a year ago said it was arthritis and dismissed me with a prescription of anti-swelling medications. Behind his thick rimmed glasses, I could sniff the judgment in his eyes as he said "Well, it happens to even the best of us"

Was it my fault that I was born fast? Was it my fault that I trained harder than anyone else in the team?

Did I buy my good looks with a bribe?

At this point I was in front of the grocery store. I caught sight of my reflection in the glass door. It was shocking to see how stooped I was and the slowness with which I tried to grab the handle of the door. I felt trapped in an old man's body. Where did it all go? The mansions, the private Harvard trained bone surgeons at my beck and call. Where did all the pretty ladies go?

I swear my heart rhythm malfunctioned just now. The thought of ladies does that to me these days. I could not help but see Kathryn's perfectly sculpted face and firm breasts as she coyly led me into the bathroom of my hotel suite. One minute she was giggling as I thrust into her from behind, the next minute she was sobbing hysterically in a room full of jurors and what must have been a billion cameras.

That's where it all went, *amigos*. The endorsements were the first to go. They were withdrawn faster than my goal against Atletico. I secretly started a game in my head to see how long Georgina will last. Two years was the answer. As she squeezed her designer clothes into her Gucci bags, all she kept muttering was "Você se recusou a colocar um anel nele"- You refused to put a ring on it.

But to be fair, how could I? Those days it was difficult to know who was in for the long haul and who only wanted the lifestyle I could provide. In any case, I never believed marriage was all it was cracked up to be. Honestly, I did not believe anything in those days except the fact that I was the greatest.

I pressed the repeat button on the music app on my phone as I handed over the hair dye to the store clerk to scan.

MØ continued against a backdrop of drums,

"...I can't believe we let it pass, we let it pass
So beautiful, but you were right, yes you were right
We couldn't last, but a blast we had..."

I almost tripped over a slight irregularity in the flooring as I stepped out of the store. I felt my phone vibrate. Only one person bothered checking up on me these days. A viscous tear drop trickled down the right side of my wrinkled face as it occurred to me that this was the one person I despised the most as a younger chap, because I felt he had a knack for stealing my shine.

I fumbled around the 'Accept' button. The caller ID read: 'The Greatest'

My voice crackled as I tried to force some enthusiasm into my speech.

"Amigos! Messi, howdy?!"

SamX

Sam X was the real deal, a daunting mixture of stealth and hairpin accuracy- A killer with a long list of kills, and zero sightings. If Sam marks you for death, you don't go to the cops. You do not try to hide. You cannot hide from your heartbeat. You do not ask the pope to pray for your safety. He is not even safe himself.

When Sam X marks you for death, you grab a bottle of cold beer, smoke your last cigar and sit in a silent park as the smoke lingers in your last breath. It is only fair that you choose somewhere quiet. You do not want your brain tissue splattering on kids playing with their balls and sunny smiles, when the bullet pierces your temple.

These were the thoughts burning in my head as I walked towards the decrepit bungalow in Agbo oba, Ilorin. It was a dream come true to be called by such a brilliant artist of death. I had bludgeoned Tunjasky's head with my laptop the last time my fraternity clashed with the bastard Eiye boys. I enjoyed the way his dark red blood splayed towards my face with each blow. I stabbed that bastard albino boy in his left eye when I heard that he was making a pass at my girl. *Person wey still dey struggle to see. Thunder fire am.*

It was only fair that people began to mention my name in whispers when death was discussed. I have paid my dues on the streets.

Therefore, when I got the message two days ago of an invitation to become an apprentice, I smoked an extra stick of Jigga's Shisha. I saved it for times like this. Next level-Sam X-Abuja-killing stuff is what I was made for. It's funny how many people gripe about not knowing their purpose in life. The day I squeezed a chicken's head with my bare hands, I knew. As its blood dripped down my forearm, it dawned on me I had found my calling. Was that so fucking hard to get?

As I knocked on the wooden door under the cover of darkness and the sound of *Keggites* dancing to Fela's songs two blocks away, I breathed in deep to take in the smell all around. I took in the clogged gutter in front of the house and the *akara* Mama Shakira was frying across the street. A small, ugly lady who looked at least forty beckoned me to come in. She had a limp and smelled of fish and sweat.

"I am the one you have come to see. My name is Sam Akpayan."

In one breath I was revelling at knowing Sam's surname, in the next I was clutching my neck as a knife in her right hand was suddenly squeezing into my Jugular.

"That's the mistake you all make. Same fucking mistake" She said very softly.

"I am a woman. And yes, you were my target tonight"

THE FOURTH WALL

Dear Seun,
1.45am, Lagos.

It was really nice meeting you today. Your voice was an orchestra, deep and lush, plus you knew all the right things to say.

I loved how you actually listened to me, and not just stare at my chest like every other guy seems to. *laughs*

Anyway, I will be more than happy to see your handsome self again.

Love,
Chinyere.

She placed her finger on the backspace button and pressed hard, till her laptop beeped in protest.

No way was she going to send such a lovey-dovey mail. It made her sound cheap. She knew her worth!

Ok, maybe there was nothing so special about her, still it was better if she at least played a little hard to get. She could not believe she was currently seated, naked and cold in front of her laptop at midnight, all because she met some guy.

But in her defence, she refused to give him her number when he asked for it. She brought up the idea of them communicating via email for now. She hoped it made her sound posh and mysterious, like the vixen of a James Bond movie.

As Chinyere got up to go to the adjoining bathroom, she caught sight of herself in the giant wooden mirror on the wall. Her breasts, like deflating brown balloons, drooped coyly on her chest. She turned to look at how flat her butt was. She wondered if there was some top shot surgeon somewhere who would be ingenious enough to take some fat from her breasts and make her butt more rounded and firmer, like Aisha's. She wondered if Seun would also call her a *double keg, no yansh,* like her classmates did behind her back in high school. She was not going to send that mail. Let him look for her. Let him fight for her...she prayed.

Dear Chinyere,
1.45am, Lagos.

Sorry to have called you chin-chin earlier in the day. Just one look at you and my words left me like a betrayed lover. It was a pleasure getting to know you. Each time you giggled, something beautiful tickled within me. I hated how loudly our mutual friends were chattering around us. I just wanted to hear your heart beat, to know it was fluttering the way you were making mine.

But Seun did not press send. Instead he held the power button on his phone till the black screen stared blankly at him. He was scrawny looking and unemployed; a depressing mix of mediocrity and outright failures. She was shapely, cute and light-years beyond his league. He desperately wanted to beg to see her again, but he knew her inevitable refusal would break him.

And so it was, in the wee hours of a harmattan morning, that two lovers did not find themselves. Their insecurities stood between them like the fourth wall of a theatre and they forgot they were the actors in this play.

THE RAID

A man stares blankly into the distance as his fingers fiddle with the buttons on his uniform.

His friend touches his shoulder.

"Why you dey do like say person die? You don forget say na ordinary police we be? If dem talk say go, we go; if dem talk shoot, we shoot. Oga no like am. Ashewo house don dey plenty pass church for area. No be so e suppose be."

"Hmm..." The man begins, "Bose nko?" His voice trails off like gentle waves getting lost in the sea.

His friend begins to laugh heartily, clutching his belly as if to stop his gut from herniating. He stops abruptly when he sees that the man looks dead serious.

"See this my guy oh! He smacks his friend jovially in the back.

"Be like say you don even forget say you be married man. With Shildren sef. You wan come tell me say you don fall in love with ashewo? See me see trouble oh. Any way no be her area we dey go"

But the man is not listening. At present he is tinkering with the cheap silver ring on his left middle finger, but his mind has wandered far from this airless room. He is lost in thoughts of how it feels when he lays his head on Bose's flat belly as she strokes his bald scalp. He thinks of how soft and warm it feels when he is buried in her member as he cups her buttocks with his hands, their sweaty bodies intertwined like roots of a raffia tree.

The man does not think of his wife, almost double the size she was when they first met. He does not want to think of the stretch marks that line her thighs like a zebra crossing. He imagines that as usual, she was currently somewhere in Apapa, hawking bottled water to angry, impatient commuters stuck in traffic.

All he can think of is the way Bose moans as he thrusts into her and how she makes him feel...like a man.

****

A woman preens at herself in the mirror as she gets ready for the next customer. Tattered one thousand-naira notes lie carelessly on the rickety dressing table next to her bed. She always thought marriage would save her from her insatiable sexual drive but well, here she was- A play thing for all the perverse things the mind could fathom.

A man and his friend kick their way into a room that smells like guilt and sin, the nozzle of their blood thirsty guns swinging edgily right and left. The man's jaundiced eyes settle on the woman whose arms are wrapped hungrily around the skinniest guy he ever saw. She turns to look into the eyes of the man, her husband, as his knees sink heavily to the floor.

Music from the grocery kiosk downstairs filter into the room. John Legend is singing like he has been here before.

We're just ordinary peopleee...

HOW TO BE A MAGA

(A 'Maga' in Nigerian pidgin English is the victim of a scam)

Step 1: Be Vulnerable

The sun was scorching hot when I stepped out of the house and made for the bus park. I was on my way to Ikeja where I had what was possibly the interview of a lifetime- not because it was my route to the senate- far from it. But as of now, it promised to be the ribbon that tied all my future plans neatly together. You see, I just finished my one-year compulsory National Youth Service, a program I reckon is a complete waste of time, unless you used the spare time it affords you to pursue some personal development agenda of any sort. One thing was crystal clear in my mind; I didn't want to practice as a doctor in Nigeria. So, my plan was simple- or so it seemed back then- get a high paying, low commitment, possibly non-clinical job, while you write the foreign exams that will save you from the rot that our health service and post graduate medical training was becoming.

Consequently, you should understand why I embraced carefree oblivion when I got a text message 2 days back inviting me for a job interview I could not remember applying for.

It went thus: "Supreme Wellness Health limited hereby invites you for an interview at 10 am, in xxx building, Awolowo way, Ikeja..."

"Call this number for more information."

A gentle breeze of doubt tickled my cheeks, so I called the number.

A young lady picked up the phone. Her diction was decent enough.

"Bla bla bla... we also have vacancy for a director of our health maintenance organization"

I scratched the pessimism on my left cheek. That was all the confirmation I needed, first a real human being was on hand to answer my call. Secondly, they had just the kind of job I was looking for. *This life ehn, sometimes you just have to work by faith*, I told myself.

Step 2: Be Gullible

So, there I was sweating profusely in my 2-year-old suit as I approached the gigantic skyscraper where our interview was scheduled to hold. I took a quick glance at my left wrist. I was about 30 minutes early.

I took in the 30 or so people gathered round the entrance of the building-an eclectic army of ants around a dishevelled cube of sugar, nervous faces also trying to size me up. It was clear we all needed whatever jobs they had on offer. I struck a conversation with a gentleman who very neatly summed up his adult life to me. An engineer (my mind registered technician), who was also a pastor (Hustler...check) and was involved in a couple of more endeavours I was too deep in thoughts to remember, being preoccupied with more pressing matters. I was scheduled to resume in the private hospital where I was currently working at about 3 pm. This was 8.30am. I'd have to leave here by 1.30pm max.

Currently my pastor-engineer friend was commenting on all the fine cars parked around the building. He shook his head as he stared at the ground before him. "God, I need this job", he said in a husky Igbo accent, his brawny hands rustling through bushy hair.

In due time we were summoned to a well air-conditioned room on the 4th floor of the building and told our aptitude test will begin in earnest. A fair skinned lady with too much make-up and a blonde wig very soon distributed our questions to us, mumbling something about how integrity was paramount to the job we were there for.

I dived into the verbal aptitude questions heart first, acutely aware that I did not prepare for one measly second for this test. To my chagrin however, I couldn't help but notice grave grammatical errors in the questions themselves. This did not feel right. It was then I realized I already had a virtual score board before my eyes. I ticked my new observation under the column marked 'Negative'. A shove of optimism nudged me continually till I marked 'Presentable and well air-conditioned room' under the positive column. The game was on.

In about 30 minutes time the test was rounded off and a PowerPoint slide buzzed into life on the wall in front of the room.

The woman who shared our papers to us initially was currently asking for our attention. In a weird high-pitched voice, she started speaking to us.

"Good day lads and gentlemen" she chirped. "Me I don't talk too much oh! I just want to tell you about this great opportunity you are here for. First remember the words of Steve Jobs who said the ones who thought...think they are... sorry, the ones who are crazy enough to think they can *shange* the world are the ones who do"

"Mr. Dayo...Ahh! Mr. Dayo...such a great man. Me I will never forget how he has changed my life. Don't worry; you will meet him very soon"

Negative ticks were flying left, right and centre in my mind. I stretched my legs before me and leaned into the chair.

"Let me tell you my story", she continued. "As you look at me like this, I was ordinary, ordinary sales *garl* in Shoprite oh! But then I met Mr. Dayo, our C.E.O and he changed my life for good. See this business ehn! You will all become a millionaire. Did you see the black jeep parked near the side of the door?" She was beating her chest by now.

"It is mine. Small girl like me. All you have to do is believe. See ehn, this life ehn! If you meet the right people and take hold of opportunities, you will make it." She brought out what looked like a crumpled teller from her purse. "This is how much is in my account now, let me show to just the man sitting here"

She walked towards a diminutive man in a checked pink shirt in the front row. Arching my neck forward, I tried my best to observe him as he stared blankly at the piece of paper she shoved in his face. He either was not impressed by what she showed him, or he did not see anything at all.

"Anyway, let me call my *oga* to talk to you" The nervous '*Ko ko*' of her high heeled shoes faded into the silence that had engulfed the room as she stepped out.

Some disgruntled mumblings swept through the room as a shuffling of feet quickly culminated in a slim, rather well-dressed lady storming out of the room as a man walked in. I reckoned he must have been the great Mr. Dayo. He was dark skinned and well-toned. He had a rather broad nose that wiggled slightly to show the disgust on his face. He looked down at us.

"Anyone else?" He had a crisp voice. I noticed a shiny briefcase in his left hand.

"Is there anyone else who would like to leave? We cannot force people to be successful". When he noticed the mutters wane like tired waves he let his lips form into a gentle smile.

"The next set of millionaires in Nigeria" He started, his cocky walk carrying his 6-foot frame from one side of the room to another. He placed the briefcase he was holding gently on a desk in the front left row.

"Young millionaires" He added.

"Welcome to the turning points of your life"

Step 3: Pay the Commitment Fee

"I will tell you a little story about my life. I finished with a first class in civil engineering from the great University of Ife" He let it sink in as he paused for dramatic effect.

"I roamed the streets of Lagos for 2 good years looking for a job". "*Two*" He reiterated, with his right index and middle finger waving at us in case we could not count.

"After one embarrassing interview after another, I met Mrs. Perpetua. One conversation with her changed my life. Ladies and gentlemen, all you need is one meeting with the right person and your life will change for good. Two weeks later after she introduced me to this totally legit business I did my first job." His smile became broader and warmer.

"I remember getting into my room and emptying a bag full of cash on the bed." He let out a squeaky laugh

"Hard cash *mehn*! I had never seen so much money in my entire life"

Mr. Dayo paused thoughtfully and looked in my direction, his eyebrows arching acutely as he searched for his next words.

"See, I do not like to talk too much. All I'm saying is that that machine over there" He pointed at his shiny briefcase

"...has dollars, Pound sterling, Euros, and any other currency you can think of in this world. What's more, when you start this business, you will be like a superstar. As in you will actually be a superstar in your community. You know the way people think doctors are like superstars. As a matter of fact, till now many people call me doctor"

I glanced at my watch. It was noon already. I did a mental calculation. I should be out of here in about an hour's time. By now, the virtual scorecard in my mind had closed as the ticks on the negative column had broken the board under its sheer weight. Right now, I was only hiding myself in this room from the unforgiving sun outside. The interaction was getting rather interesting anyway. Here I was 2 years post induction into the medical profession and I had no idea I was a superstar.

Mr. Dayo motioned to one of his subordinates who stood transfixed at the door, marvelling at the smoothness of his boss's words. The man, bow tie and all, briskly walked to the laptop that was connected to the projector to begin a slide show. The first few slides contained quotes and charts from the works of Robert Kiyosaki, but they soon faded away to reveal Mr. Dayo in what looked like a hotel out of the country, swaddled in a snow-white bathrobe. Other pictures showed him in the same bathrobe just outside the hotel with two Caucasian women in office clothes smiling sheepishly at the camera.

"You see, you will be called doctor," He was saying, "Because you will not only be making money...lots of money, but also helping people's health at the same time. All you have to do is write a contract to any organization. It can be your church, or even where you work- and ask them to book a date where you will use this machine (he pointed at his 'magical' brief case) to run tests on them that will tell them everything, I repeat, everything about their health free of charge. Then you will be able to sell some supplements I will give you to correct whatever problems they have."

I swear I almost fell down in mirth, bent almost double when I heard those words. I have always heard people talk about a certain machine that you simply put your hand into and it diagnoses everything about your health. I'd be stupid to claim I knew it all, but basic knowledge about the science that goes into the design of medical tests, and the sheer structural differences between different modalities of investigations makes the validity of such a test, at least for now, questionable. An MRI (Magnetic Resonance Imagining) worked in a totally different way from a CT scan and gave a very distinctly different set of results. The reagents used to run a thyroid function test was more different from those used to perform a full blood count than Buddhism is different from space travel- they weren't even in the same category.

Thus, I was sure that if such a machine really did exist Nobel prizes would have been won over its manufacture and governments would throw banquets if they could purchase one for their state hospitals.

"But first" Mr. Dayo's deep voice brought me back to the room

"You know the saying that no pain, no gain. You have to pay an enrolment fee before we can enlist you officially into the program.

Look, I am not forcing anybody here. You either want to be rich or you don't."

"Our gold members have to pay a tiny sum of 100 thousand naira to get the gold package." He again looked in my general direction. I'm guessing it's my suit that was causing the attention.

If you are interested, please put up your hands so Mrs. Nkechi here can talk more to you in the other room."

I stared at my watch. It was some minutes past 1pm by now. I began to put my things together.

He gradually reduced the fees until about 20 thousand naira- I think that was the bronze package- when three enthusiastic hands shot up.

As I walked out of the room, I could feel his piercing eyes on my back.

He was explaining how all these dues were simply commitment fees, so they could be trusted with the machine.

"See, in this life *ehn*, nobody can force you to be a superstar" he growled with sarcasm, his small eyes piercing into my back as I shut the door gently behind me.

CPSIA information can be obtained
at www.ICGtesting.com
Printed in the USA
LVHW032056230122
709171LV00002B/16